THE KNIGHT HAS DIED

OTHER NOVELS BY CEES NOOTEBOOM

THE KNIGHT HAS DIED

A NOVEL BY CEES NOOTEBOOM

Translated from the Dutch by Adrienne Dixon

LOUISIANA STATE UNIVERSITY PRESS
Baton Rouge and London   1990

Copyright © 1963, 1965, 1982 by Cees Nooteboom
English translation copyright © 1990 by Adrienne Dixon
Originally published in the Netherlands in 1963 by
    Uitgeverij De Arbeiderspers as *De ridder is gestorven*
Manufactured in the United States of America
First printing
99 98 97 96 95 94 93 92 91 90   5 4 3 2 1

Designer: Laura Roubique Gleason
Typeface: Sabon
Typesetter: The Composing Room of Michigan, Inc.
Printer and binder: Thomson-Shore, Inc.

Library of Congress Cataloging-in-Publication Data

Nooteboom, Cees 1933–
    [Ridder is gestorven. English]
    The knight has died : a novel / by Cees Nooteboom ;
    translated from the Dutch by Adrienne Dixon.
        p. cm.
    Translation of: De ridder is gestorven.
    ISBN 0–8071–1544–4 (alk.paper)
    I. Title.
PT5881.24.055R513   1990
839.3'1364—dc20   89-13622
                                                   CIP

. . . un autre but de l'homme, plus secret sans doute, en quelque sorte illégal: son besoin du Non-achève . . . de l'Imperfection . . . de l'Infériorité . . . de la Jeunesse.

—Witold Gombrowicz, *La Pornographie*

THE KNIGHT HAS DIED

1

His devastated life. What a task: I am to commemorate the life of my friend the writer. Here beside me on this table lie his papers. Notes in inconceivable chaos, half-finished poems, diaries, fragments from books. And I knew him, which does not make it any easier.

He is dead. I find myself in charge of a ridiculous piece of trickery: I have become the overseer of his deceit as I finish the book he was writing. I do not need to invent a plot; he has already done that. His book was to have been a book about a writer who died. Another writer finishes the dead man's book. A simple idea, like the nurse on the Droste cocoa cans: in her hand she holds a can on which is depicted a nurse holding . . . And so I sit here, with eternally receding writers, mine and his, who die with other writers at their heels who then complete their works, but who die, etcetera.

Why am I doing this? Because I knew him? That is not enough. There must be another reason. He was more than his pointless death, more than the bad, or at any rate unimportant, books that he published during his lifetime. I venture to complete the attempt at rehabilitation that he clearly intended to make. He and I will have to accept the resulting lie as part of the bargain. To speak in his terms, I have decided to "erect a memorial for him on his unseen grave," which yesterday, at the cemetery in Barcelona, I narrowly succeeded in avoiding.

I shall have to conduct my business with much forethought. Today I start with his Hero's Memorial Day. He is called Our Hero. André Steenkamp, author. Author.

A life of no importance, tormented, but by the wrong things, and with one single love, or what passed for love, which finally, when the time had come, emptied his life. I weigh what he left behind, all those papers, the endless repetitions, the contradictions, pathetic cries, documents of impotence, and a helpless insight into his own situation. His only strength was that he understood how things were with him. Out of this insight he wrote, or rather took notes. He never got around to real writing.

He died before he became a writer, or because he had to become a writer but could not. That, too, is possible, after all. His handwriting is always ugly, too tormented. And however much he left behind, it is never enough. I shall have to cheat, put my own imagination to the service of his noisy fragments, supplemented by what my (so much healthier!) powers of observation have noticed about him, and then add extracts from the many anecdotes concerning him, for I have made my inquiries. Only out of the crudest opportunism would anyone erect a memorial to such a person. To think of it! I shall even have to write "he said" and "he thought"! He would have done better to leave his papers to someone else, to one of those industrious toilers who will publish them after twenty years, complete with biographical and technical annotations and footnotes. I know that many times I shall feel ashamed of what I am doing to him. But thanks to the temporary German thoroughness that I have adopted for his sake, I shall finish it in the hope that at least for one moment his tottering shadow will rise, recognize and commemorate itself, collect the ashes, and then vanish forever to the realm of heroes, to that wonderful domain where knights ride on horseback in brass armor to nowhere, glittering in the sun and singing at the tops of their voices. No doubt about it!

2

In the month of February he steps ashore on this island. It is the month of the witches' sabbath; rumbling rains are making the roads impassable.

He had arrived in Barcelona by train. The old white ship of the

Compañia Mediterránea waits for him and then abducts him. The legend begins. Am I still speaking of him? Is he speaking of himself? Am I describing him instead of his protagonist, who he was also, but to what degree? And I? The sea is green or gray or black and is being lashed with whips. I have no desire to use *all* his metaphors—some of them are in the vein of the sea that was as green as a cat's eye, and, then again, a color as vile as absinthe. Similarly, his "wild Russian coach drawn by a team of twelve" (the ship). The rain lashes him in the face, but he likes it. The night is "broken in half," and in the "vast gray halls of distance" there looms the shape of the island, an apparition. He is sensitive to the legendary aspect of such arrivals, he is excited, his pale face is raised heroically. How long ago did he first hear about the island? I was there. It was at one of those pleasant gatherings that so frequently enrich our nation's literary world. I saw the word, the name, enter his consciousness. The next day he had already bought a map of Spain, and he pointed out to me the route to the island, across the blue sea, the ferry route a thin red line, the line along which he is now, together with dolphins, Russian carriages, and excitement, being drawn toward *his* island.

A man comes up and stands beside him. Or rather, I place a man beside him, but with the consent of the events as they happened in reality. A drunken patriarch in consecrated tweeds—although Maugham, for he came from that stable, would have described him differently. His heavy trousers are held up by a multicolored, woven belt, fluttering gray-white hair, eyes drowned in a wide sack of a face, and those eyes yellow, and sick, scanning the horizon with their worn-out radar. When the island appears on the screen, a kind of joy breaks out in the hills and valleys of the face; he rattles against the rail with his impossible walking stick and says it is beautiful. Very, very, very beautiful. He says it to André with great emphasis. It is very beautiful, the island.

And then, the overture. The booming voice pours it over our hero—his name, his admiration for and attachment to the island. Everything in a slow and very emphatic English that does not fail in its effect. Yes, it is beautiful, says André, it is beautiful, it is beautiful, and he thinks how nice it would be to float above it, lie on top of it, because it happens there, the house *happens* in which he is going to live, the bed stands there in which he will sleep that night, the people happen whom he will know. (This was my first *he thinks*, and I notice I am not finding it easy. But I will drum it into them. I cannot do this with impunity. Especially not if, in his idiom, I have to make houses and people *happen*. Even if you are prepared to accept that as his reality, you are still not obliged to write it down with pleasure. All I am now doing is making it clear that I don't. After all, he died of those exaggerations. The only reason, for the last time, to remain faithful to him.)

The voice of the man beside him pollutes the day with Moors and Phoenicians, Greeks, sites where wine jars and oil flasks have been found, inscriptions, irrigation systems. The tenth century, eighth century, the island grows older and older, wantonly old, a barricade full of dusty graves and sacrificial caves, dominated by the moon, the white goddess, by the Moors, bombed by Mussolini's planes, the bishop disguised as a peasant woman fleeing inland from the anarchists, while his brother is shot . . . It affects him, together with the rain, with the wind of that morning, together with the hills that he now sees more clearly.

In the blackness of the distance a vague greenness has appeared. He also sees bare yellow patches, sometimes rocks, a hint of red, terraced fields, and later, even under the woolliest green, traces of bare earth, just as the shape of the skull is sometimes visible under an old woman's hair. Specks of white, houses. Things that move, a small boat passing a rock, growing larger.

The man beside him, the initiator, leans toward him and says his name for the second time—Cyril Clarence. "There are *many* Dutchmen living on . . . did you know that? Hah hah, you don't like that, do you? Hah hah, a complete Dutch colony. Hah hah! Let's have a drink and spill some! *As a libation for the gods!*" This phrase lingers in his mind, I can testify to that. He meekly follows the old man to the bar, holding onto the rail. The encounter does not justify his growing feeling of excitement, he thinks. But the excitement takes no notice; this is the first part of the game that is being pushed toward him, Cyril Clarence the first of the saints, the first member of the court. And he has accepted; he is already playing.

The bar is full of early-morning statues, their beards frozen to their faces. They are the poor deprived saints who spent the night outside on deck, a monastic order without possessions, eating dry bread and onions, or bread and olive oil, tasty with pepper and salt. There are many saints here, saints and demons, sent by the somber, general will of a collective spirit to this island, which is reputed to be an island of saints.

The Englishman envelops him in a woolen cloth of stories and fables, pointing with his brown-colored finger here and there among the statues, and André absorbs it all. The island, the island. Like a real writer. He still sees nothing. They drink absinthe, and through the portholes in the bar the shore draws nearer. Cyril points and points and spits out names: Cala Pada, Punta Arabí, Cap Roig, Cala d'en Serra, Platja de Talamanca. Suddenly he says, "Another fifteen minutes," in a tone as if he has just come. Then he stands up heavily and sings, "I'll see you at the quay," and walks away, leaving André in a fragrance of holiness, the thick low-hanging smoke of a brown cigarette. Ideales cigarettes. *Ideales!* The statues around him creak and stir. He is beginning to feel afraid—we shall see this more often—and goes on deck. Close by now, a fortress, high up on a hill. The boat turns slowly around a pier and enters the sheltered harbor. He will not be permitted to forget the vision of this arrival; caught in a Renaissance painting, he watches, and the bare skull of a town looks at him, a tall, triangular pile of white houses with open black eyes, the place of skulls topped by a medieval church, ancient sand.

I don't want this, he thinks, I don't want this. On the quay people stand waving and shouting, and from the ship others shout back. The islanders on board have come out of their holes, and their voices wash over the foreigners who have now become the minority. Vital messages, call-notes, children are born and the dead are buried in those calls, whole families are plunged into mourning or made happy with a rustic and long-awaited bridal bed, and he stands by the rail as if about to bless the multitude, but the messages and events pour over and past him, they do not concern him.

He sees the stone quayside edge toward him. His map has become reality, no longer yellow and bordered with red, but gray and rain-soaked. He is being jostled by everyone, suitcases and cardboard boxes push and shove him, the ship knocks against the quay wall, once and then again, everything teeters—the beginning of a Saint Vitus' dance—the gangplank is put out and shock troops of blue men with numbers on their caps swoop down on the ship shouting, "*Mozo mozo!*"

One of them follows him to his cabin to fetch his suitcase. It all happens very quickly now, as he leaves the safe enclosure of the ship. The quay smells of people; other journeys suddenly leap at him, hurried films full of steaming trains waiting at platforms, magic voices from loudspeakers telling truths, and always the execution of the sentence: a taxi, the hotel room filled to the last corners with carefully prepared silence.

Mozo Number 11. The unshaven face under the far-too-large cap talks. He has to listen. *Pensión? Coche? Sí, sí.* Shouts and handclaps. This car is at least thirty years old, he thinks, and at once he himself becomes older (everlasting swindler), stiff and cold and with a haughty past of colonial service, colored houseboys, whist drives, gout. He gets into the car, two steps, his pale hand loosely cool in the strap, looks through the dirty glass pane at the driver's neck. There is no need to talk. The *mozo,* his private chamberlain, provides commentary, explains. I want this to last forever, he thinks. A man getting out, turning a handle, the jolting and then the plump, old-fashioned throb, the power of 1929, Lili Marlene, an apocalyptic war, brakes. This car simmers gently on the fire, tugs at the air outside, begins to move, conveys him. The town glides past the windows, men in black, women in local dress, and among the people the scarce saints who frighten him with their beards and other holy signs. He doesn't want to look. The car climbs. (But all of this is overture. For God's sake get on with the story. Of course. His emotions in a car of this sort. And the gates of the town, and the harbor.) A Roman gateway, double wooden

6

doors as thick as centuries—he wishes they would close behind him, then he could withstand any siege. The streets become narrower, the car drives over sand, and at every turn the harbor has dropped farther away, an anecdote. Deep down in that green bath lies the ship on which he has never been. Suddenly it is finished, the car stops by a low house, a bowed old woman is waiting at the door, the men speak to her in the dialect of the island and sentence is carried out: the room is low, the walls are gray with damp. Above the bed hangs a Jesus scarcely able to bear his pain. André drapes a handkerchief over it and says, "Horrid man."

There is no washstand, only an enamel bowl on a little wooden table. In the pitcher beside it there is water. He walks around the room and listens to his footsteps. Seven to the window, and there lies the town again, a cascade of houses down to the harbor, then on the other side a narrow strip with a lighthouse stuck in it, behind it another bay, shadows, hills. To the right there is only sea, almost the one on the map, but moving against the rocks. To the left the hills never end, behind them, in them, there teem secrets, witches, sheep, peasants, deliciously odorous fig trees. He smiles to himself in the mirror in which he does not see himself, whistles, sings, and shudders.

The old woman knocks on the door; she has come to ask if he needs anything. A glass of water. She brings it and as she watches curiously he lets two split pink pills drop into it and drinks it up. "Bye, Mother," he says and gently pushes her out of the room. Then he undresses and slips between the hard rustic sheets on the brass bed. Beneath him seagrass creaks and rustles; it rocks as if the slow sucking of the sea were still pulling it this way and that, a tepid and languid fanning in the silent halls. He is asleep.

Oh, those dear old-fashioned novels in which it could be written: we shall now leave our hero for a while and go to A., where at this same moment the secret of his life is being unveiled. He sleeps, and veil after veil falls from his face, leaving it naked. Behind the closed eyelids the fluor-colored eyes move back and forth, looking at dreams, and what does he see? His arms crossed in front of his chest, he holds onto himself tightly, protecting himself. From what? From me, who now pervades him with his own words? But they are only words that do not go fast enough for my liking. I hate this first stage, and I have to refer to my loyalty again, in order to declare that I shall keep this up, this slow, naturalistic narrative across which I constantly and impotently see his pathetic figure, beleaguered with fears of the most childish kind, someone who suffers. And I must not exhaust him, shout out the future to him that I now know. No, guided by his hand, clutching his papers in my hand like a true fetishist, I must continue to follow him in his story. In order to cover up his shame at his youth, which is nothing but a feeling of guilt because he has lived, he uses the simple addition method, which is easier; it shows him to be assembled out of so many different photographs that he himself has become lost. But even to say this is a form of distancing, so I give him back to himself. He is (this is literally what he wrote) his accumulated happenings, they have crept into his hands, have given a color to his eyes, shaped his mouth, they speak with his voice. But the relationship between them can never be recovered. This sometimes surprised him, that he was every minute of his life and that so much of it had escaped, been wiped from the slate, vanished into lost time, scrapings of his growth. All that was left of it was a number of explosions, noisy memories. From his childhood no voices, no toys—only his parents' bed, the smell of which, one morning, had penetrated him once and for all. Of his father no voice, no sound, only some silent film. A drunken man knocks the top from a table with one blow. He hates all the photographs from that time—he has no authority over the child who stands there, he would not recognize him in the street. It is a dead person, a creature that no longer exists. Three photographs later he is five, six years old. And slowly (this is work) the ugly, too-old child in the photograph, a stolen moment, a stolen copy of part of the sum, dangerous, seems familiar to him.

The eyes have been touched up, and something that he remembers has also been added to the mouth. Events, two. One is the immense sackful of planes being shaken out over his house. He lives near a military airfield, and for two days the planes fall, blacker and blacker, over the house. They wail, burn, and dive time

8

after time above the too-green summery fields behind the house. Everything he touches in those days trembles—and he knows that his father therefore hates him—for as long as the air attacks continue he trembles; cold water is of no avail. And this is almost the only memory he has of his father: a man who has a chair placed outside for himself on the balcony, where, smoking in silence, he watches the fighting. After two days it is all over, and after two more days his father takes him out, and together they watch the Germans enter. The street is wide, the people standing along the sidewalks are silent, and in the middle, in the beautiful middle, the endless gray army rolls and rattles past.

What connection does this have with the sleeper in the brass bed? Where, in which corner of his body, do those burning planes now crash, where is his mother beaten, crying, where does his father leave the house with mute gestures? Everywhere memories gather, crowd together, always present, always powerful. Shall he allay them by writing about them, or shall he spoil his writing by those so frequently displayed, obligatory attempts at hygiene that have nothing to do with *making*? But all right, he need not worry about that, I do it for him, for my friend, even though, as hygiene, it comes too late. It won't open the way to real writing for him anymore. (This hits the wrong note again. And the right one.) And the other things that no longer belong anywhere, bits of street in no city, a beach without sea, a meadow where hay has just been cut. He reads a book in that meadow. The book no longer exists, but every meadow where hay is cut will later be only that meadow. Every blue sky will be only that blue sky, which has carved itself into him, once, somewhere, never to be recovered, or as he puts it, "drowned in a throat of fat clouds."

The photographs become more and more recognizable. It is time for him to start hating them, they come so close, intrusive, convinced of being in the right, of their right to him, of their rights. Their right to make him enter wide, green-painted Limburg gateways flanked by worthy monks in brown habits, getting up at a quarter to six every morning, swarming into chapel, bodies fractured into the kneeling position, praying, praying. There he stands, looking at himself in the camera, as always, the full, pale faces of the monks suspended around him. The writer at school. Cavalcades of cheerfully charging memories come running toward him, that whole self-willed world without a world, vocations, confessions, plaster heads of classical writers lined up in bare corridors. His mouth is stopped, and when later he wants to open it again as a writer he talks through a layer of sugar, unintelligible even to himself. In sour-smelling confessionals, lines are drawn between his childish onanism and quite different people who have died on the cross for that as well as other reasons, and when no one is looking, quick, into that hole and pray, preferably on the bare stones, it has to hurt. He was like that even in childhood. The lives of the Saints, and frequently talking to God, and Oh and Ah, I will and Thou knowest, and if it is not Thy will, I have, but perhaps it is Thy will. A velvet stalemate later on, he will forever boast that he has experienced it, but that Catholicism has had no effect on him. No effect on him! And the endless sessions with the friend with the huge head behind the organ, sweetly warbling ribbons of Bach, no effect. And the weeping with the poems of Van Eeden under the trees, no effect. And there was always time to take photographs. He becomes ever more foolish and ever paler under the prescribed green cap. Around the corners of his mouth appears his first novel, the position of his feet suggests his tamed, latent aggression. The writer he wants to become flutters helplessly inside his body, and you try to get out of that if you can. No, when I look at his face and consider what it has become: nothing much has changed, a few strengthening layers perhaps, plastic, to preserve him better. I have by now caught his hysterical tone quite well. Those strangers standing around him, where are they now? Are they turning this way and that before altars, muttering in a secret language? It may be so; anything is possible. Sprinkling water over hard skulls, stroking fuzzy pagan hair with consecrated hands, judging. Are they thinking of him? They have the same photographs, after all. Look, there is Steenkamp.

But he had his auxiliary troops, too: the evening peace in the gardens, the scents of evening. Mist hangs, cool, above the football field. Outside the walls a dog, a car, the bells of the monastery across the road. And early in the morning everything very light and clear, and the cold air of the morning peaceful. Every leaf has been brushed with water and so also smells of peace. The walks to the marshes, sometimes, on free afternoons—and time swallows it all up, miles of peace, all at once. Dusty country lanes, painted trees, reeds, brackish marsh water, armfuls of flowers that even after thirteen years still go on blooming, falsely and dry, in the faded cemetery of his herbarium, named and labeled. Every minute of it was valid, was a minute that could not yet be looked at from a point in some future, could not be made ridiculous by a later, autonomous time.

Threads, images, phantoms, shadows. The valid time that once existed, that has lasted as long as the time that exists now. Gone where? Later he will be able to make up stories about it— "the first time I had to serve at mass I felt ill"—but what does such a statement mean? Can it reassemble the smell, the time, the sounds? Those memories and those stories, what can he do with them? They are not the cold morning in winter. They are not the half-crazy old monk, mumbling and burping as he prepares to say mass in the little chapel of the German nuns who cook for the monastery. Nor are they that group of alert nuns who, "blown out of their beds long before sunrise, sit wedged tightly in the wooden pews, on cautious knees, spinning prayers and thoughts, sad troglodytes."

He has helped the old man put on his chasuble, and together they make their way on small Caucasian ponies to the altar high in the mountains. He crams his mouth full of Latin, and the monk and he blow it toward each other, phrases meet on the steps on which they kneel, the old man climbs, speaks, turns and returns, and then he wants his hands to be washed, he wants wine in his chalice, and then he wants to kneel and pray and turn it into blood, drink it, the nuns want to come to him, want hosts. Now everything glitters at once, the glass cruets in his hands, the golden chalice, hollow and curved just below his eyes, the hard, prickly gold stitching on the chasuble, the monk's plump scaly hands making the sign of the cross over the host, over him, over the birdlike nuns. But then it all becomes too much; sobbing and trembling, his waxen face with the light-blue sparkling eyes thrust

11

into the wind, he flees from the altar where the priest suddenly remains dreadfully alone, blessed amid the nuns' tormented sighs. He runs through the corridor and flees into the garden. His punishment: he will never be allowed to serve at mass again, the only boy in the whole school so excluded.

3

He is asleep. Where he is it is still February, rain and wind against the window. Where I am it is June. On my walk this afternoon I saw a field where the wheat had already been harvested: it smelt of bygone times. I swam with my snorkeling mask on. It was cool down there in those immense spaces, seaweed moved, fish glided slowly and soundlessly past me. Rocky caves studded with sea urchins and red anemones, fields of sand wrinkled as Saharan dunes. A happy world. I wove my way through it in total silence, flying above meadows and abysses, in my irrepressible happiness landing from time to time on coral islands, waving to fish, diving at hermit crabs in their borrowed shells. I felt a strong desire to lie down on the seabed, relaxed as a dead body. But he is dead, I am not.

How far have I got with his portrait, with the statue I wanted to erect for him? What have I said, whom have I described? And for God's sake, what is true of that mythical shadow-play I set up, those memories, the deceitful maneuvering of his fears, photographs, vague sentiments? How many scents, peaceful evenings by the water, childish torments have I forgotten? Was he pathetic, or do I find him pathetic because he is dead? Or because he is a dead writer? I have the desperate feeling that I am pushing with both hands against a solid mass, tough and dangerous, which will concede nothing. His corpse is becoming bigger all the time, and no matter where I look, I cannot recognize him anywhere.

Threads, images, shadows. He comes flying wounded out of his school, into the world that embraces him clammily. But there is always an antidote (against mistrust, lack of talent, overblown

12

images of loneliness) that can be drunk with much sugar; endless crates full of nature, carefully unpacked, recorded, catalogued, ornaments in the collar of the tragic countryman. Forests, the sound of trees, ponds, rustling, the moon, the moon, the moon. He will feed on it for years. No people, no thoughts, not even himself. Daily pilgrimages to places of natural beauty, the consecration of trees and streams, poetry, and not of the best kind, swallowed to the point of suffocation. The arsenal is inexhaustible, green water, Mediterranean Sea, palm trees and cypresses, long strands of poetry without reality, without bones. This is how I find him, this is how he found himself, with a deadly shock, but too late. Filled with fear but without knowing of what.

4

He is not allowed to go downstairs yet. The effect of the two pink pills has not yet worn off; their strength still flows through his body, dragging a heavy, slow dream behind it. He lies in the bed, clammy and tossing. I sit on my terrace, there is not a soul in sight, Homeric shades sway and break in the archaic light, no one ventures outside. The windmill on the hill creaks and screeches at every turn of its large sails. That and the sea are the only sounds. I sit and wait.

A rowboat glides slowly through my memories. A man is rowing me to somewhere. Who is he? He has no face. I know where this is. To my left glitters the bright green water of the ocean. It must have been two years ago, in the North, in Galicia. A ferryman is taking me across a river; I am his only passenger. On the other side burns the bank. Why does this memory come back to me now? A warning, but against what? The man must have made an impression on me, because of his appearance, his voice, a gesture. Perhaps he was singing. But his face has vanished. I shall never see it again. The boat moves away, taking me with it. I remain behind empty, caught between the voracious hours. What better can I give them than my friend, whom I no longer recognize? I have maimed him, like the Poles maimed the SS colonel who lives next to me here, a bloated man, his face full of craters, crusty scabs, and amiable Bavarian slopes, amiably stitched up. Now André must go down. Somewhere among the mutilations he himself has caused and the distortions I impose upon him, I must find his clearest shadow and send it, laurel-wreathed and kissed, to the land of heroes, for that is what I want.

5

He wakes up. He doesn't recognize the door. It is roughly painted; where the paint has been applied thickly there are now small cracks, and in other places the wood shines through patches of mildew. There is a handle of battered, mottled iron, hanging loose in a worn, ragged hole. The wall that has grown around the door has been whitewashed with irregular brush strokes. Damp gray stains, holes left by vanished screws or nails, a restless surface approaching and receding. He lies in bed looking at it, not participating in anything.

The house behind the door is silent. He sits up, the light flees, the wall recedes. He quickly gets out of bed and puts on his clothes. In the town that hangs beneath him, the lights are already burning, the ship, whose whiteness he can still see through the dusk, hisses steam and whistles. The water surrounding the island like a force is black. It glitters—the moving light beyond, farther away, must be fishing boats, he thinks. He can hear the muted throb of engines. He straightens the bedclothes, puts on his raincoat, and gropes his way out through the dark corridor. It is cold, the wind races. He debates whether to turn right or left, chooses left, descends all those steps, crosses muddy streets, arrives at the harbor. The wind is even fiercer there, it leaps among the people on the quay, chases the ship out of the harbor, skims tauntingly over the water, against the current, and through André Steenkamp's hair. He walks along the quay. Everywhere there are low, dark bars where fishermen play cards, uttering wild cries. He doesn't know where to go.

"A bad place to write in," he sings softly, "a bad place, a bad place." A broad avenue lined with palm trees, light from old-fashioned, silver-painted streetlamps, in the middle a statue that has become crazed and cries out to heaven. He sits down at a terrace and, truth or fantasy, a towering figure with a dirty white fluttering mane and inflamed eyes comes swaying toward him. This is the man I have chosen to initiate him. Actually, I don't know much about his early days on the island—a few rough notes indicate that he had been all over it. At any rate, when I met him (an encounter of which I shall be careful to avoid mention in these pages) he had already been initiated—so why not by Cyril? I still have a weak spot for him and see him affectionately settling on André, taking possession of the precious stranger, besprinkling him with anecdotes, spinning a cocoon of stories around him. His costly, well-groomed doglike head leans sideways, the ineffably cultivated voice tells endless tales in the evening air, the eyes are always somewhere different, flutter about, alight here and there, know nothing.

It must therefore also have been Cyril who took him to Pepe's that first evening. That is the correct order. Domingo (clean Domingo) at the end of the afternoon. He is there now. Then dinner at the Formentera or the Bar Bahía. Coffee at the Estrellas and then to Pepe's. When that bar closes, back to the Estrellas, among the card-playing fishermen. The last port of call is the Alhambra, the very last one the Bagatelle. The morning always starts off at Domingo's again. Everything is bound by rituals; sainthood, once again, is here hardly attained in isolation. O golden days!

Pepe's. He can find them all there, his armored tea party, the Ring of the Nibelungen: Gordon, Nescafé Jack, Helmuth, Schramm, North, Ingmar, Nitribitt, Vicente, the two Antonios. But there are too many of them, far too many, and to him they remain shadows those first few days, although Cyril points and whispers names—the names and stories of that bizarre tribe, muttering or silent, perched on the uncomfortable stools, waiting for big, ugly Pepe to take up his masterful guitar again and scratch the strings with his iron nails, sst, sssst. The autochthons chuckle.

Like a failed satrap the lame man sits on a wooden bench, his embittered face chiseled against the red cloth hung by his wife on the wall of the cave.

He wears black clothes, one of his shoulders is higher than the other, his face is emaciated, sometimes sad. The most terrible diseases are attributed to him, including membership in the secret police. A small black moustache embellishes his face somewhat. The divine instrument rests on his wooden leg. He lifts it. Silence melts among the beards. André peers at Pepe's hands; the thumbs especially are gruesome and not fit to be seen, owing to the torture-nails.

Cyril has greeted the man exaggeratedly in order to stress his status as a regular, and they sit down as close to him as possible—but everyone is always close enough to him, for on the bare walls hangs his portrait, twenty, thirty portraits, all of them bad, and rightly so, for no painting except a bad one could adequately represent that arrogant face. Some are painted in dirty red, with small, rigid, magic eyes, with wooden Pepe-sorrow, always and everywhere that same staring image, become incarnate in the middle of the cellar, and—how could it be otherwise?—making music. No wonder that most of the women drink *hierbas* here, a green, thick-looking juice that burns in the glasses and is kept in large bottles full of twirling evergreen plants from the hills. Such drinks are drunk in temples. A half-dangerous, grubby religion hangs in the air, but even the master does not know that.

They stay for an hour, then a group of Cyril's faithful followers splits away from the crowd, takes leave of Pepe with fond hand-shakes and pinches on the arm, the master beaming and whisper-ing valedictions from the husky speech-issuing corner of his mouth. Headed by Cyril, the small procession wanders about the narrow North African streets. The wind tugs at their clothes, they swerve round large muddy puddles, sometimes the moon can be seen skipping among the clouds. There are conversations, but André does not yet take part in these; he sees mainly himself walking in this mysterious casbah and smells a novel. They go to Antonio's. Good, he thinks, they go to Antonio's. Even from a distance, they hear the dull African rumble of the local music. Our hero opens his mouth slightly and looks magnificent in a pose of happy admiration: he had not expected to be so fortunate.

16

At the heavy wooden gate, the good Antonio produces his strange rigid laugh, and out of mysterious black depths he digs slow German phrases of welcome and friendship. What is shown to them is touching. In a corner of the cellar sit four old men. One has a little drum hanging from his left arm that he beats with a stick held in his right hand. With his left hand he plays a three-tone wooden flute. The music is wild and tragic; it revolves in long insistent circles on the monotonous, sometimes passionate African rhythm of the drum, becoming fiercer and louder when joined by the clattering of the oversized castanets and the ancient sound of metal on metal held by the other musicians. The music soon conquers everyone in the cellar: the eager, staring eyes of the strangers isolate the men in the corner, an isolation that increases whenever dancing or singing begins, bird songs and bird dances that have nothing to do with anything, unrecognizable, archaic sounds, and at the end of every phrase a terrible bleating tremolo. No one present belongs to this music. André doesn't either, not *he*. Slowly and inexorably he is driven away from this cellar, this antiquity; even the silence, when the rushing of the music stops, does not bring him back. He has vanished through some crack in the wall, this knight, and there he also hears, no, *sees*, Cyril's voice beside him, with a hundred echoes. The face has been hung in front of him ten times too large, the ears have ridiculous lobes, long wattles of pink, polished flesh that quiver as he speaks, when he says, "Once I was in Oxford, in a *pissoir*, and you know, on the wall, in the most BEAUtiful italics, it said 'Dylan Thomas slept here' (beoootiful italics it said Dylan Thomas slept here) WHA WHA WHA." The mighty laugh chases away the bird music and resounds back and forth around the cellar. For the first time André really sees the man, and from that moment on he will listen to every story, every day, until the last story dies in that mouth, for that is what will happen.

The music has started again. The harsh old voices bleat their new animal songs into the deaf strangers' ears. Is it about love? About the moon, goddess of the island? You cannot tell from the fishermen's faces. The others recede further and further. André sees how they slowly hide behind their own shadows. He wants to get away! Fear grabs him in his stomach, turns him about. To be left so

17

alone, already! This is not why he has come to the island. He thinks of something complicated like . . . my external boundaries are tightened as by a vise, I vanish from within, but he has already dropped out of the metaphor, he calls Antonio, has just time to say goodbye to Cyril, who stays behind, surprised and incredulous. Was this a leap, taking him suddenly outside, alone into the muddy street between the low white houses, into the silence in which soon not even the last fleeing sound of the drums is still audible?

Fear, insane fear. He walks in the direction of the harbor, everywhere a knocking and thumping of engines. Sound at least. The fishermen leave the harbor. Stamping, slanting, the boats sail away, dark shapes hunt with round yellow lights. He climbs up on the pier, toward the lighthouse, in order to follow them. He can still hear shouting or long hoots of music before they vanish on the invisible sea where it hisses and blows. He envies them because he does not belong. For God's sake, to have something to do, catch fish, come home with something, not with that slovenly, humiliating fear of which he refuses to think. The only thing he can think of is writing, and it almost makes him vomit, but he keeps repeating the word, keeps it in his mouth, poor idiot. He lies down full length on the wooden bench by the lighthouse. Time after time the light sweeps its silvery, pointed hand over him, and he tries to adjust his breathing to it. When the light is not there he sees the heavy, coarse clouds passing low overhead, now and then scattered apart by the wind to reveal a fragmented, deranged constellation, a ruined Orion, a mutilated Great Bear. After a while he becomes peaceful, he begins to feel cold. He tries not to think about writing, and then he does try to think about it—as of something he can always do in the future, something that will happen all by itself, the truth that will reveal itself and will therefore absolve him. Absolve him from what? Another thing he must on no account think about. But there will come a time when he will no longer need to hate it, the way he hates it now, as a weakness, a deceit (he thinks). He gets up slowly, clothed in himself *as in a pose*, and walks down the pier, a character out of a novel, this novel. In the village, among the white houses, he finds the road up through the

Roman archway, and wending his way through streets and alleys, meeting no one, he suddenly finds his lodging house. Sitting at the small wooden table, he tries to write something down—a sentence, an idea—but a total helplessness has seized him, scribbles appear on at least twenty sheets of paper, on which he then spits and makes smudges. He reflects that he is now all alone in the room. I am alone in the room, does that mean anything? He digs a manhole in the bed and buries himself. Not until the first gray slivers of real light penetrate does he fall asleep, a clumsy, crooked heap under a quilted blanket. I do not know what dreams threaten and preserve him now. Worriedly I go up to him and look. Some of the (narcissistic) solicitude he had intended for *his* hero has now infected me. But how much more tenderly would *his* writer have looked at himself? And how do I look?

6

Sometimes, on a misty Dutch morning, when you are roaming on the heath and an invisible, distant huntsman fires a shot, the short clear explosion describes, no, writes, more clearly than ever you could write, a feeling of happiness: I am alive, I am alive. That is more or less how it is, he thought. The morning was of a barbarous, sharply cut brightness. He stood barefoot on the red tiles and looked at the hundredfold face of the sun, across the fishermen's quarter, across the water, across Talamanca, the golden strip on the opposite bank, across the emerald marsh in which lay dead ships, the revolving, assailing sun like a shot of light in the veering sweep of a flock of diving birds. He got dressed and went out. The Spanish air, bright and transparent, surrounded him like cheerful water in which the colors glittered and the sounds had a pure, ringing clarity that in the North, he thought, you hear only in specially built rooms, never outside. Never, never outside.

Yesterday, a drab, dejected, lingering day with the wind scratching like chalk on a school blackboard, and night falling, low and somber, raising no expectations, and then suddenly the new day, open and shrill, filled with light and sound, every minute bursting with exuberant peace and joyfulness, the mouth of heaven wide open, thrusting out a breath full of bright spirits. Only here, by this sea, long trumpets are raised toward the sun and blow across the water, over the fishermen in their colorful boats, against the brassy cliffs and onto the land, stirring up shepherds and their flocks in olive groves that tremble in the heat, and pressing wine from the grapes.

He had to make an effort not to run the last lap down to the lower town, straight from the tall archway to the marketplace where the black-clad island women stood among their wares, bright green peppers, long strings of rusty *setas*, red tomatoes from Valencia, hard yellow lemons, the stiff light green local lettuce, still dotted with clear dewdrops. These women had come from the interior on high, rattling carts when it was still almost night, in black shawls, still night themselves, chattering to one another in their secret language. *Cebollas, naranjas, pepinos, setas, manzanas, limones, toma, toma hombre, está muy barato todo!*

He now finds the road to Domingo quite easily, past the rigid three-masters in the harbor. He has himself shaved by a dwarf. *Masaje? Si!* Set it on fire! Half a bottle is poured over his face, then the little hands pummel and stroke, his face is made to conform to the great Mediterranean happiness outside, a cloud of insect powder against misfortune does the rest. Forever protected, he goes out, ready for anything. He alights like a dove on the chair Cyril has kept free for him, in the shade under the palm tree.

Dear Cyril! an elderly gentleman out of a fashion magazine, *peau de suède, Prince de Galles,* a necktie by the late Jacques Fath, and drinking small bottles of champagne, Pitel-lo. Four or five empty bottles stand and lie on the table in front of him, and his beloved Vicente is already bringing another. "André! I have been waiting for you for ow-ers, old man! Do have a Pitel-lo." Lovingly his fingers stroke the frosted exterior of the glass, and then suddenly he sits very still, as in an old daguerreotype, as if he could sense he is being robbed of something. And he is being robbed; lock, stock, and barrel he vanishes into the voracious head of the writer, who is already using him and who therefore despises himself. You are not allowed just to sit here, thinks André, it is not allowed, you are sitting next to a writer, you are being robbed, I take what I can use, a yellow eye, a ridiculous habit, seven bottles of champagne before eight o'clock. Presently I shall jot it down, and that makes me into a thief instead of a friend, the way it always is, thief instead of lover, thief instead of foe. Don't think about it. He orders champagne, although he knows it doesn't agree with him. An hour later there is no room left at their table. Characters out of novels, not people. The palm tree under which they sit now casts its shadow in the other direction. They are sitting completely in the light—dappled with light, the actors sat in the immense limelight and said . . . Is he lying again? What has he actually seen of all this? Surely he didn't see, couldn't see, what was there? Those laughable steps back and forth in time, which ignore, distort everything that is real.

At the table: Gordon, Nescafé Jack, Philip North, Andrew Schramm—paladins grouped around the immortal composer Cyril Clarence. But to him who sits among them, looking through narrowed eyes at the unfamiliar, dust-covered oleander across the road and at the unfamiliar silhouettes of the houses and at the unfamiliar door of the Compañia Mediterránea, they are mere names. Never again will he see the faces that he sees for the first time; or, never again will he see their faces for the first time. What he sees now are the crude, unfinished shapes, the raw material out of which he will fashion them. A snatch, a shred of Gorley's shrill RAF voice, the leaden, invincible figure of Jack who puts his own Nescafé in a large glass and asks for hot milk, the crumpled oriental face of North on which New York has played havoc for twenty years, the giggly shadow of Schramm's genius, hovering like a languid, invulnerable bird above the conversation.

The sentences, their remarks, the small openings behind which a glimpse of soul stirs at times, the moving picture of their faces, a glimmer in North's spectacles (he too is a writer), Cyril's Jacques Fath necktie—it all marches through him like armies through an empty hinterland that has been conquered by the vanguard the day before. He sits there and does not stir. His eye, that huge organ, is busy, uplifted by the champagne, and there is also, on this bright morning, the scent of hashish. When the morning makes another quarter of a turn, he slides out of their tableau and walks down the long, long street, because at the end of it he has seen the hills.

The heat quivers above the road. It must be near noon now. His steps are jaunty and almost floating, and somewhere he takes a right turn. On the stone wall bordering the path there still lies the mud of last night's rain, but the path leads to the wild hills in the distance where the sun stands straight above the red soil, skips between the gnarled olive trees, and shoots long, sure arrows of light at the low Moorish houses, into the green fields full of waving tobacco. At every crossroad he opts for the hills, and an hour later he is there and falls panting in the sharp grass amid the stones and looks back for the first time and sees the sea, the town perched on the hillside above, the olive groves, the green salt lakes like saucers of poison. The light hurts his eyes, it comes so close, and he hears the music that would accompany this landscape in a movie: soaring *pastorales* with striking bells and an invisible choir of a thousand women with feathery voices. He rolls on the ground as though trying to find a spot to lie down forever, but restlessness and too many stones drive him farther, and puffing, he climbs without stopping to the top of the hill, among the swaying pines. The view toward the sea is now wider—beyond the salt marshes he sees low hills and a long white beach, behind them once again the sea ablaze with light. When he turns round and looks into the land, the hills continue, undulations with green, humped backs as far as he can see, and in that arrested movement he is the seeing center in which an immense silence is suddenly born. Set into motion by the light, the entire landscape whirls around him. It is as if he were being drawn apart, as if the truth about him were being written with a steel pen.

It passes so quickly that afterward he is able to think calmly, "I am dizzy," and he sits down carefully, like an old man, against a tree. It is so totally silent around him that he wonders whether he has shouted.

Why is it happening already? Happiness evaporates from the landscape, it is thrown away, and when a little later he returns to the town he is merely an accidental person in a picture postcard.

To either side of him flows the cardboard, colored landscape. You just cannot see his fear.

That same day he leaves his lodgings. He has learned to manipulate his fear, to bargain with it, he knows that by means of a few small changes, a different house, walking out of a restaurant during a meal, he can postpone his departure from the island for a while, until, in a larger game, he can shove this also toward his invisible opponent, toward his fearful self. The painter Schramm welcomes him affectionately; there is etiquette among saints, after all. He has a large old house outside the town, on the cliffs. Good Antonio (*Wie-geht-es-Ihnen-Ich-sehr-viel-Weh-am-Kopf-immer-viel-Weh, Schmerz*) helps him carry his suitcases and typewriter; he doesn't have to concern himself with anything, merely wanders through the dark smugglers' tunnel that runs under the thick fortress walls to his new home, where the sound of the sea will never leave him alone anymore.

In Schramm's house he must have had an opportunity to make a start, however small, on his book. And of course his famous notes, with which I have to work. He stayed a few weeks.

7

The morning of the long day. The sun shines in the waves. From the cathedral on the hill the clear sounds of bells float toward the balcony where Schramm and André sit together, two conspirators from a court drama rocking in their rocking chairs like madmen. "Last night," says Schramm, "I dreamed I had been commissioned to paint the sky. I remember that I was about to start working on it, with a grim kind of relish, thinking of only one thing: how I should paint the sun. I decided to paint it right in the middle of the picture, and I mixed a white color that ate away all the other colors. But guess what . . ." He takes a deep breath. "Each time I was about to start on the sun, a hole appeared in the huge canvas, just at that spot. I woke up, my hands in a cramp, and I started painting." André had already seen the painting but had not dared make any comment. It was a luminous field of force, on which the word *sun* had been written in at least ten different places. SUN SUN SUN SUN SUN SUN SUN.

Schramm turns his chair toward him, bends his hawk-face over him, and asks. "Why don't you write? You don't do anything at all, you go to your room, you scribble, you get up again and walk away, you sigh, I can see it, you come out of your room looking pale, it's bad. You must work!" Those are Schramm's confidences, uttered with sighs, but useful. These memories were clearly not sufficiently heroic to be preserved by the writer himself. A fraternal rebuke does not add much to cosmic despondency. Nonsense.

André gets up and walks to the edge of the balcony. Schramm watches his thin, slightly stooping figure and wonders whether it is the sun that makes those eyes look so strangely, luminously blue— as if they were glass eyes capable of holding all the light in the world. The face around the eyes is disadvantaged as a result, weak and vague, a face that deliberately resists emotion. Or tries to resist. The writer walks all the way along the edge of the balcony and returns to Schramm, saying, "I can't write." Schramm: "Why not?" "I tell lies when I write. Or I have no life. Either my life is real or what I write is real. It is a distinction I cannot . . ." The conversation drifts away across the glittering sea. Schramm starts to chuckle softly and rocks harder, then he raises his tall, birdlike figure and with flapping wings walks into the house to crouch by his gigantic painting. Now no one is allowed to speak to him. Sometimes he sits there for hours, peering at his paintings, as if he were flying above them looking for a prey hidden somewhere down there on a passionate ground plan.

Once André asked his permission to add something. The painter nodded yes, and somewhere on the edge of a purple, tumorlike explosion, André placed a small servile wisp of yellow. With judging eye he took a step back to assess the effect, but took fright when the painter rose, menacing and vengeful, streaked purple all over the little yellow curl, and then forgot him again, as now.

For a moment our hero pauses irresolutely by the studio door, sees that the painter, withdrawn into his work, has become uncommunicative, and leaves the house via his own study. In his room, papers are left lying on the table. He decides not to take the muddy road into town but to climb over the hill instead. As usual he tries to reach the top without pausing; panting, he stands on the crest, looks down on the great platter of the sea, finds the white house he has just left, and thinks of Schramm who is now working in that African cube. *He is making a picture.* A feeling of shame and envy assails him, and he turns around with a jerk, kicks against the large cactuses that grow there, and then rushes down the hill on the other side, uttering wild satyr shrieks that startle the sheep grazing under the olive trees.

From the village come brassy cries of march music, people are thronging in the direction of the Vara del Rey, the main street, where the music comes from. Moving with much difficulty through ever-denser crowds, he reaches Domingo's terrace.

8

Here, too, excitement reigns. Cyril is dressed as for a boat race. He no longer has that decayed, inflamed air about him; he sits like a polychrome statue between the worn figures of North and Nescafé Jack and tips his chair back and forth from sheer joy. "The day of the AHR-MY," he calls from afar and points at the snappy officers parading down the broad central lane, surrounded by women and children, large purple sashes across their chests, splendidly bemedaled, gold leather belts around their waists, high gleaming boots.

"Now look, it is a fiesta today, a fiesta of the AHR-MY! Now just look at the lovely things!" Even the most barbaric soldiers wear white gloves with their mud-colored rags, the commander of the marines passes by in bridal white on which an iron cross carries simplicity to its extreme. He greets the foreigners condescendingly with his baton, and North pulls his most hideous grimace and says, "Fuck Franco, Señor Comandante!" Nods of acknowledgment.

The confused events are coming to a head. The general feeling of happiness has imparted itself to the foreigners, at all the tables the sun shines in the Pitel-lo. More and more people crowd together at the corner by the cinema next to the Alhambra; across the street, the officers enter the muddy building of the military command. Policemen in drab blue uniforms come to clear the road in front of the terrace, and a moment later a group of about seventy soldiers marches by in silence, preceded by a bugler and a small band that is not playing. The last six soldiers are carrying the silver-plated tools of the engineers on their backs, a silver spade, a silver mallet, a silver pickax. They come to a halt in front of the building. Suddenly it becomes very quiet. All the officers are inside.

A jeep pulls up and out of it jumps, breathless, fat and covered in medals, the island's military commander. The first few bars of the national anthem. Silence. The commander salutes the colors, enters. A little later he re-emerges, followed by all the officers. Nothing can be more beautiful, thinks the writer, when in total silence the forty primped-up officers with sabers and cheap sunglasses and the most improbable medals stand opposite the troops, seventy men in all. The silence is unbelievable. The faces portray an expectation gently fanned by the merry whirr of an old car somewhere in the distance. Everyone leaps to attention. A low-slung, very old Citroën with a brightly colored pennant edges round the corner. "Oh! My heart!" Cyril whispers into André's ear. The car stops in front of the troops, the commander plunges forward and holds the door wide open. Out of it steps, trembling and shaking, a very ancient, purple-clad bishop, sunlight in all the jewels of the cross on his chest. He stretches out his bony hands to the commander and whispers something. The commander's neck is fast turning red from bending over. Briefly they hold each other in a whispering embrace as though in a tremendously secret council, then they simultaneously let go of each other and, wonder of wonders, do not fall. Again, the first few bars of the national anthem. The commander takes the bishop into the building; there they commit the perfect crime, then reappear with a glow of grand drama around their shoulders. Now a whole anthem is played, and the commander, panting for breath, sets himself in motion and strides the length of the troops, as slowly as possible because there are scarcely enough troops for the duration of the anthem. At the end of the line he stands very close to André, who briefly looks into two watery caves full of faded military discipline. He clearly hears the man say, "*Está bien!*" There is a flash of sabers, and once more he inspects the line, his spurred boots slishing across the asphalt, nods to the standard, to the bishop's purple blur on the sidewalk between the gold lacquered hat of the commander of the Guardia Civil and the officers' gold, purple, and brown. It is over. The crowds draw a deep, rapturous breath. The bugler, small as a fly, makes his bugle blare as for a big hunt, everyone pivots a quarter of a turn with a sound like a gigantic sob, and the column starts to move, wistfully watched by the officers who then trickle back into the building for the reception.

As André and Cyril, arm in arm, arrive back at Domingo's, the group around their table has grown. A bloated pudding with sculptured sideburns and brown leather knee boots is there—Alaska Ben, the poet—and next to him a small, fat Frenchwoman who pulls André onto the chair beside her. "I live above you," she says. "In the morning I often see you sitting on the terrace." He looks at her face and finds it hard not to push her away. She briefly lays her short plump hand on his arm, scraping his hand with the long dirty nail of her little finger. A soft white trail. He withdraws his hand and goes indoors. There is no one there, an old dark station at which no train will ever arrive again. He peers at his white, silvery face in the advertising mirror, and it is as if he were looking straight through his own eyes. Far away. It's getting worse and worse, he thinks. Jesus Christ, I must do something. He goes on peering into the face. Is it afraid? Nose, mouth, eyes, are they afraid? He cannot tell. It isn't me, he thinks. A gasping fear takes possession of him, the dizziness that always follows it hits him at the back of his knees. "I must think," he says aloud.

An old man, Domingo himself, shuffles in through a door at the back and looks at him from behind the bar. "*Qué hay, hombre, no estás bien . . . Quieres algo?*" "*No, no, gracias.*" On the movie screen before him, against the bright light coming in from outside under the raised bead strings, he sees it clearly, the panacea, the tremendous remedy: I must murder that fat girl. Then it will all be over.

Afterward, the blessing of friendly landscapes. He himself, having discharged his murderous task, suddenly invested with the new dignity of an excellent equilibrium, walking along a well-swept asphalt road on his way to, at the very least, the horizon. Domingo brings him a glass of tepid water, and in order not to disappoint the old man he drinks it quickly and then walks out, blind as a mole in the light. His victim has vanished, and he promptly forgets her. Everyone is standing. Has he already murdered her then? "Oh, André!" Who, where? Cyril, of course, at the edge of the picture, he holds out a long hand into the light . . . "We are going to San Vicente! We are going to the holy grotto of the moon goddess! To Astarte!" Schramm—but where has he sprung from?—carves a threatening shadow toward him through the light. "Today is a day of prayer," he says gravely. "The taxis will come here for the pilgrims. First we'll go to Santa Eulalia, then to San Carlos, and after that we'll walk because the road doesn't go any farther. That is more fitting for a pilgrimage anyway. Come with us, and pray for inspiration." And he blows into his face, a little puff of holy spirit, by way of advance. André watches him sail across the road to the place where the taxis stand under a long row of palm trees. In great suspense a large circle of islanders follows the negotiations between the *locos* and the drivers. Fifteen minutes later, the first taxis pull up alongside the terrace; there are at least ten of them. André squeezes into a small old Fiat with Cyril and North and a fat Irishman who is rumored to have been castrated in a war. Amid shrieking, hooting, and the hysterical waving of handkerchiefs and fake sobs from the direction of Domingo and Vicente, the taxis turn their noses toward the harbor. They are on their way.

"The taxis of the Marne," whispers North and pulls the cork out of the brandy bottle with his teeth. They all take a swig. The Irishman lies back and gurgles. Cyril's head flops sideways, and he falls asleep, burbling words and fragments of sentences from time to time, conversing with someone who is not there.

On their right, the green marshy corner of the harbor recedes, where dead boats lie stuck among the water plants. They turn inland. At the end of a short plain of farms and windmills rise the hills; the road runs straight toward them. The driver has wound down the window, and the scent of the countryside wafts in, pulling at their hair, blowing across their faces. The Irishman sings softly to himself and does not answer when North asks him a question. Close in front of them there are two more taxis. Every now and again a burst of raucous song rushes in, and a moment later all sounds are dashed by the bleating horn of a large Buick that wants to pass. Schramm and Alaska Ben lean out of the window, two characters in some devilish masque, Ben flushed and red, a degenerate angel, and Schramm hissing and screaming at North, "Filthy dirty smelly useless American Writer!" North, immediately filling his Jewish-Chinese-Slavonic face with rage, shouts back, "Filthy stupid worthless American painter! You never sell anything!"

Bellowing, the big Buick overtakes the other taxis as well, the two heads shout insults, and other heads now protrude from all the taxis, flushed bright red from shouting, hair streaming. The driver shrieks with laughter and tries to make his old Fiat catch up with the Buick, but it is already far ahead, a gleaming beetle in the distance, hooting sheep and Roman chariots off the road, climbing toward the hills, whose dull green falls apart into untidy pine groves that have in some places been pushed back by low white farmhouses on small patches of land hacked and conquered from the stony ground. In front of the houses, peasant families sit in low wicker chairs and watch in bewilderment as the screaming, hooting procession passes.

"And years later they'll still be talking about it," says North. "'Do you remember that day when the foreigners drove past in more than ten taxis? They were all drunk, ha, *borrachos todos*, and they grabbed the women in the cars, you could hear the women screaming, *los gritos de las mujeres*.' Maybe it will become a popular song." He raises his voice into a false flamenco tune, "One wi-hinter day . . ." The Irishman interrupts him, "On the day of the a-harmy . . . *a-hal día del Ejército . . . los taxis . . .*" Cyril tumbles out of his sleep straight into interminable laughter and whispers between gasps, "This island . . . is a paradise." A huge pothole jolts them, and they grab hold of one another and sing with long leaping wails, "It's a long way, to San Vicente . . . it's a long way . . . to go . . ." And André joins in and thinks why don't I join in properly, why am I thinking about singing? Are they also only thinking about singing or are they really singing? The driver's face is bathed in happiness, he sounds the horn to the beat of the song, joy bursts out of the taxi on all sides, André bawls at the top of his voice but his eyes continue to photograph all the faces in the shamelessness of their joy. Joy is not-looking, he thinks, and with his eyes shut he bangs with his whole weight against the wall that separates him from the singers, yelling like a madman, shrieking in a child's voice until the song dies away in its thousandth repetition and they let go of one another and take swigs from the bottle and light their Ideales.

"Look at that landscape," says North. "Pay close attention, writer, it reeks of gods and history. Under all those olive trees, behind every miserable hillside, there lurk childish little gods gone crazy from neglect, their little faces purple with envy, sticking out their shriveled little tongues at the passing cars."

"Hoohoo," he calls out the window. He turns to face André so that the sun is reflected in his double lenses, and it is as if André is being looked at by a shrunken monster with big round eyes of glittering metal and the monster jumps and shifts with the movements of the car and hisses titteringly, "You just try it, you just put on your fucking wooden shoes and buy some milk and apples and shuffle into the *campo*, in the middle of the night, and put your offerings under any tree you like; the next morning it's gone, gobbled up. And if you're brave enough to stay, oh God! You'll see. Then they'll come with their misshapen powdery heads and their twisted little crawly legs, you'll hear them coming from a distance, creaking at the joints like a thousand crickets, scraping across the ground with longing, screaming for offerings, a gruesome procession of drooling *dei loci,* abusing one another in extinct languages, Phoenician, Egyptian, Greek. They hardly have legs any longer, with their elbows they paddle their divine shanks to the place where you are waiting and you smell their bad breath, the stench of their immortality. They are addicted to prayers and adoration, but when they have finally devoured your measly offering, pulling each other's hair and poking each other in the belly, only then does it really begin—they crawl up to you like dogs, dogs that nobody wants to touch anymore, they lick your feet, their bodies jerk and thrash and they want only one thing, one: that you pray. And you pray. Anything goes, prayers for the weather to change, or please may I never get cancer, or spare my mother for many more years, you throw in anything, and they start writhing and gasping with pleasure, ten gods, thirty gods, a hundred gods, one huge deformed neglected god's body, screwed for one last time on the corner of the crumbling altar!"

He tweaks André's nose. "You don't believe it's true what I say, do you? I can tell. Ha!" The iron, the contemptuous fingers let go, André shrinks back from this hatred, but North's head pursues him into the corner of the taxi. "You're wrong." Briefly, slyly, the short broad tongue licks the lips. "Put your head out of the window. Well? What do you think you smell? Peace? This is no peaceful island. There are more gods here than there are rabbits. This is a concentration camp of frustrated gods with a hundred names to whom no one ever prays anymore. Have you nothing to live for any longer? Does life seem empty and without purpose to you? Then take a ticket to the peaceful white island that lies in the ancient sea like the moon in the sea of the skies. Hundreds of gods bursting with immortality await you, sucking at eternity. They will be more than grateful for your visit."

He leans back exhausted and puts Cyril's hair in front of his eyes, squealing with laughter. The Irishman sticks his fat castrated arm out of the window and points into the distance that is suddenly, because of a bend in the road, hidden behind the landscape, a valley, gold, a stream, a village, a high hill on which white Moorish buildings glitter in the marble light, Santa Eulalia.

9

They storm down the slope, and with the same speed the village rushes toward them. Cameras, tape recorders, everything is busy, and meters of sentimental film nestle in the backstreets of his brain, and he can play back this entry over and over again: the line of cars, descending in front of them, over the golden saucer down below, and then, in formation, crossing the old Roman bridge under which the ribbon of the river stretches as far as the sea. Boys smaller than the reeds are fishing there, they wave to the taxis. Cyril waves back with the languid arm movements of a royal dynasty in decline and says he wishes there were *thousands* of them.

"If I were in that crowd, I would throw a bomb at you," says the Irishman. "Made of the most expensive plastic, too good for an Englishman, really." He adds a curse.

André sees how a small red wave washes over the cheeks of the dog-face, but now they are already swerving into the village street, shadows of tall plastered tombs on either side. They stop in front of a cream-colored kiosk in a spacious area like a clearing, sand under tall trees. There is a terrace with wooden chairs. Schramm is already sitting there with a woman and a Spaniard who is apparently attached to her. He pushes his way toward them through the crowd of screaming and bottle-waving pilgrims. Schramm introduces him, and he hears her Dutch name, sees that she recognizes his. Later he recalled the exact tenor of that moment, and that his first thought was, this is . . . all the women I have known or have wanted to know rolled into one, and he also knew that he could not detach himself from this memory, which began almost simultaneously, because one second after the introduction this introduction had already become history, something to reflect upon, how from that first second they cunningly began their conquest of each other, and in this memory she was still sitting there, had not moved. Behind the silence that stuck in his ears, he heard the ranting of the Irishman and the shouting of Spanish voices, perhaps also the howling of Cyril calling for him, but that all happened behind a wall, the Spaniard and Schramm were half-drowned, only she sat there, her green eyes eating into his. He noticed that he was using Schramm in order to talk to her, words that had nothing to do with the moment and would later be swept away like so much impermissible debris.

A shrill crowing close by his ear: North has sidled up between them. He kisses her and puts his square hands before André's eyes and says, "Don't look at Clara, she's no good. The disastrous Siren of Santa Eulalia del Río, *la más hermosa,* the snake-eating Lady of Our Lady, dangerous for writers, she puts her teeth into your bright soul and sucks the essence out of it. You'll find out!"

André tries to push the hands away, but they press him back into his chair and the voice slowly trails away like that time when he had his operation, he lies under a snowy cap and the doctor's voice ripples around him, it is low tide, the voice ebbs away, farther and farther, and he cannot go after it, he becomes an immense gisant through which the blood still flows, he will never catch up with that voice, nor does he want to, and he sinks away in his sudden comfortable silence until the shell of sound bursts open again and the noise returns swelling slowly.

She stands over him and says, "You fainted."

"No," he says, "no, no." Not another word, but he is already empty and at her mercy, in search of affection, and they both know it. North stands in the background, the malefactor in the wings. His face is pale, but his voice is crowing again. André hears him deliver a lecture in which he is called "the famous writer Pacelli," and is being asked about the Other Side. "The famous writer Eugenio Pacelli has just made a VOYAGE to the Other Side, for our Spanish listeners, *el otro lado,* Hah! And he is willing to give us some of his impressions. Now, Mr. Pacelli, sir, would you please tell us how it really is out there? And a terrible belching out of visions begins: Mr. Pacelli tells us, Mr. Pacelli tells us." The Spaniard comes up to her, asks her something, but she shrugs her shoulders. André sees him walk off and come back with a glass of soda water. He drinks it like a sick man and sees also how North, still talking, comes toward him and kisses his hand, which causes him to shudder so intensely that he is scarcely able to control the urge to scream. He stands up, blessing them, but now Schramm is shouting at North, words to the effect of, you're jealous, you'd be better off not being here, even if only for a moment! Nothing could be simpler, someone brushes a hand across your eyes and you vanish! Meanwhile our writer is working on his own images: it is only the fear, melting for one instant. And of course a hundred other pictures. Fear, which then becomes benign, like a blanket, from there it is only a millimeter's distance to the next one: a child being tucked in by its mother, the feeling that follows next is that of the fear congealing, freezing, the chill all over the skin, the shivering, and for one moment all these clear "thoughts" really exist. She watches how he drinks, catholic hand around a glass, raising it in a well-bred manner, luminous eyes in a too-unfinished face, not a man, mouth corners full of gray histories.

"Are you coming to San Vicente?" She nods.

"A little prayer will do us good," says Schramm. "It gets rid of the sloppiness."

"Or call it thinking. That sounds better." He turns to André. "Do you ever think?" There follows a monologue about thinking and *seeing*. North, wearing a new armor, reenters the battlefield and calls out, "Painter! You're becoming a bore. Painters should not think. If you don't stop that twaddle, I'll steal your paints. Or I'll mix them with shit."

Schramm gets up and points his long dry finger at him and says, "You yourself are the example. There isn't a story of yours in which anyone thinks. You invent stories and then you look at them. You see images and you describe them, you're a tedious draughtsman, a scribbler of pictures. There's nothing to them, nothing." And with a slow, elastic gesture, as if he had been specially wound up for it, the painter rises from his chair, his oblong head slightly bending forward. And he disappears swayingly in the crowd.

Taxis begin to hoot, the shouting increases, a great excitement surges among the tables, pushing everyone upright. There is a jostling toward the taxis, a struggle to get in, and with coughing noises the first cars are already leaving the village street, on their way to San Carlos.

Cyril waves excitedly with his colorful belt and pulls André into the car. They make themselves as small as possible so that she can get in, too. The Irishman's monstrous head, redder than ever, falls asleep on her shoulder, smacking and mumbling. North carefully pulls the cognac bottle out of his hands and lets the driver drink.

The road is straight and monotonous. On both sides red

fields, a red that hurts his eyes. He takes a few swigs from the bottle and notices that he is gradually getting drunk, and he wants that. Cyril sings a Bach cantata, male and female voices all mixed up, and then starts crying.

"England is crying," says North. "A fine mess. What is the world coming to? Russia number one in space, America slowly rotting away in its own juice, and England crying in a taxi to San Carlos." He points out of the window and shouts, "Europe! Europe!"

The Irishman lifts his head in his sleep and curses him. "Go fuck yourself." North blows into his face and whispers, "Yeats, old chap, don't worry yourself about it. These are hard days for us to get through, us artists. Western civilization." André registers what he says, not really listening. Her hand has crept across his back and is now scratching his neck. He tries to look at her, but she has turned her head away and is looking out, her profile marked against the ancient landscape.

North puts his arm around the driver's shoulders and whines in his slow, drawling Spanish, "*Yo me llamo Scot Feetxjerald, soy muy conocido en los Estados Unidos . . .*" He turns round and twists her head so she has to look at him, "Zelda, darling, don't, not with compatriots! Did you know we are on our way to Boston? This is . . . *veinte y ocho, the year. I . . .*" He puts his head on the back of the front seat and falls asleep or pretends to. André notices that the driver is smiling at him in the mirror, and he smiles back.

"What are you thinking?" she asks.

He thinks: I am not thinking, I am working. I drag this whole moment inside me, I am working myself crazy. This is the beginning of a long story. What is it going to be? Suddenly he takes her hand, rather grimly, and feels it. The slightly rough fingers, narrow between the knuckles that jut out hard and sharp. He rehearses her face, doesn't want to look, wants to know it by heart, her mouth, her green eyes. What kind of face is it? Old at any rate, and voracious. It is always the eyes that do it, big and flashing, directed at him, and, with their urgency, dominating the other features of the face: the corners of the mouth, the moistness of her lips . . .

Her hair is dyed crazily, blonde, streaked with dark. The

nose . . . go away, nose, he doesn't want to think anymore, and therefore looks and sees simply a straight, classical nose.

"Why don't you say anything?" Her voice turns to him, after having been with the three sleepers. "I can never sleep in a car, can you?"

They look at Cyril, who has acquired a new dignity in his sleep, that of an almost dead person.

"I love him very much," she says. "I love people who are no longer quite there anymore. Sometimes when he is very drunk I think, now he is going to die . . . no one can afford such an absence . . . but he doesn't want to die. He goes around in that ridiculous old body of his. Bodies! First there's air, so that's emptiness as far as we're concerned, then a layer of clothes, and then a body inside that. Some parts of it you can see. And then that is a person. It would be so much more logical if we did not really exist, if that gleaming or dilapidated thing wasn't all we were . . . Do you like bodies?"

He shrugs his shoulders. "We are nothing but our bodies," she resumes, an undertone of drink suddenly sounds clear in her voice, something obstinate, which bothers him. "Nothing but. When it's gone we're dead." This word she cherishes. "I never understand it. Sometimes I try to imagine that the space I now occupy will then be empty."

She puts her hand on his face. "I feel you. That's you." She taps on his cheekbones, tap, tap, and smiles at him. "For something that will have to disappear anyway, it's very strong. But the fact that it will have to go . . . Sometimes I see myself decaying very fast." She smiles amiably as she says it, like a grandmother telling an old story, a tale full of wisdom. "I shrink, I crumble, my hair falls away through my jaws, I fold up, and my thoughts jump out like air from a flat tire. But it isn't quite like that, not quite."

North slowly raises his eyes to the center of the pebble glasses and says, "Mach ksach rrapher zoch zammen. Can't you two talk a more civilized language instead of that morbid Germanic dialect?" And in the same immense languor that has taken possession of André he says it a hundred times while his face is being sculptured monumentally, for a gigantic statue, the first speaking statue in the world, not only North, all of them, a huge, monstrous statue of a taxi, this taxi, and in this taxi-shrine immortally preserved, the flavor of this one second.

Can't you talk a civilized language? Never, never will it be like this again, never will he say it while they sit here with him, gods and heroes from a saga that has just begun, Canto I. The wanton autonomy of the moment assails him while the moment itself is still expanding and they sit as if in a soap bubble, waiting for the explosion, waiting while they grow slowly until the moment has completed its saga.

He thinks we are such a large statue, that no one will ever see us, in the largest square in the world a taxi so large that the people can walk in the tread of the tires as if through enormous rubber tunnels and in the taxi the taste of our life as it now tastes, and he leans over to her and says, "I am so immortal you have no idea, I am immortal, so immortal."

A cramped ecstasy shakes back and forth inside him with the jolting of the taxi, and while the alcohol courses madly though his veins he thinks I see her as though I were photographing her with the whitest light, and she poses in absolute stillness, this is again an extension in which I see her, I look into her eyes, in the center of the white lies the green stone, her real eye—with which she looks at me, she fires her look at me through the barrels of her eyes and I don't care, shoot me, look at me, I am here, I exist!

10

San Carlos. In the touristic afternoon stands a rustic white church with a low porch under which the air is suddenly cold with shade. The drunkenness, she, the others, the dark box camera of the taxi, break away from him, chilly and alone he stands by the lumpy whitewashed wall and lets his forehead rest against it. A slow circling. He looks round and sees how the others slide into one another, a large chattering crowd that must be hated.

Holding on to the wall he walks to the wide green doors. They should be open, he thinks, the house of God is always open. The

Master is there. And calls you. *Adest et vocat te.* Calls *thee.* He opens the door, looks back to see if anyone is following him, and enters.

"Here I am again," he says aloud. It booms. Mary, caught in stiff plaster movement, follows his grotesque ritual in dismay: tearfully he bends over in the farthest corner and vomits, groaning and gasping between the waves that come heaving from his stomach, like that time when he almost drowned in Biarritz and each new breaker swept him into a different direction, always farther away from the shore, and the people waved to him from the beach because he had raised his arm into the air for help but they thought he was playing a game, yes, playing a game. It fits, it fits, he thinks as he sobbingly turns and walks to the stoup and dips his hands into it, then, wet with holy, consecrated water, he slaps them about his face, and through the veil of his tears he reads the plump, confectionery-like embroidered letters on the shimmering plush altar cloth, *amor omnia vincit.*

Her voice comes toward him—"What are you doing?"— across the empty space that swivels the sound around and throws it at him. Doing? He sees her coming toward him, very clearly, a slim woman in tight-fitting black trousers, white blouse. Her face he has seen before, and he says to it, "I am sick." But he forgets her again, two armies of memories thronging together, the beach at Biarritz and the monasteries of his youth, and the images follow one another so quickly that he breathlessly staggers out of the green sea and drops down on the sand, I was almost dead, but before he is able to get up and join the girl who is waiting for him further along, he is standing once again in the all-devouring emptiness of the monastery where Gregorian chants bite into the soft underbelly of his soul. She wants to pull him outside with her but he resists. "Not outside," he says, "not in the light."

He goes up to the altar, genuflects, and turns left to the Lady chapel. The stone movie star stands with her foot on the moon and lets her gaze glide over him as she has done so many thousands of times before.

"The mother of God," he says to her. *Madre de Dios!* Candles five pesetas. *Limosnas. Pan para los pobres.* "Shall we give some money to *los pobres? Ah, los pobres pobres.*"

He lights one candle and puts it as close to the statue as possible. Now it is really becoming too much for her and she turns away. He follows her at once, but halfway down the aisle he bends to pick up a votary picture that he shows her. A light blue Jesus, seated under a bunch of grapes, one bare foot on a marble step on which there actually lies a lily, raises a very tiny host (but that is Himself!) to an impeccably dressed little Spanish boy who waits to see what will happen. *Oh María! No permitas que se marchite la flor de mi inocencia. Recuerdo de la primera comunión de Juanito Canevas Noguera. Recibida en la Iglesia parroquial de San Carlos. Festividad de la Ascensión, a los diez años de edad.*

She holds up her hand, and he puts the picture into it. Then she pulls him outside, but he wants to look back once more and points to the statue by which that one candle is burning busily, and he says, "That statue has been there for as long as I have been alive." And what does that mean? With pathos he invents something like, "I diminish merely because that statue has been standing there all this time, independently of me," but he is unable to discover in this thought any reality that can be explained, and moreover a new, much more colorful statue of Saint Paul has now drawn his attention and he reads aloud what it says underneath, painted in wavy words: *"Recrearse en el Señor siempre y, de nuevo, digo, recrearse."*

Softly repeating *"Recrearse, recrearse,"* he finally follows her outside. He no longer seems a conquest to her.

11

Outside, tears came into his eyes from the light. I am still drunk, he thought. She stood behind him and pushed him through the crowd into the wide dusty square in front of the church. Vaguely he saw familiar ships passing by, North, Cyril and a huge man he had seen before in the town, Goldstone, who tried to stop her, but she said something to him that André could not hear and came along with him to a small bar.

It was cool and quiet inside. They sat down on crooked wooden chairs by a small round table on iron legs, with a marble top rimmed with shiny metal. The marble was cold to the touch.

He rubbed his hands over it and then held them to his eyes. An old clock cut up time with dry sounds, and he looked at her and thought, every second you lose some of your precious strangeness to me, and it becomes clearer what is going to happen. He saw their hands clasping each other, and he saw how they would lie in each other's arms and how that same hand that now lay here, unfamiliar and absent, on the gray flecked marble, would stroke his skin.

"The end of the film," he said. No, he had said nothing, and the same churchlike silence weighed emphatically on their heads, and he saw the images passing before him faster than ever, how he would lie in a bed with her, but it would have to remain unclear, unclear—more than the vague white movement of bodies he did not wish to see, otherwise it would not happen.

He stood up restlessly, holding his hand commandingly on his stomach, which was sending him the forerunners of an approaching depression, small rolling cramps that he detested. As he walked up to the green and white tiled bar, he hastily popped a pill into his mouth. "Get to work, you," he said swallowing it and imagining the little white disk slowly descending to calm things down.

What nonsense, he thought, it's myself that is sick. And what is sick? How can someone tell from his stomach that he does not exist, or not sufficiently? "Is no one coming?" he asked.

She got up and walked to the back of the bar. He heard her knock on a door somewhere and call out something: *"Oíga, oíga! Señor Miguel! Miguel! Hola . . ."* Of course, nobody will come, he thought joyfully. At last it has happened, the world is beginning to empty, as it should. She returned, followed by an old man.

"You're looking very strange," she says. "What's the matter?" And she thinks, how is it possible that someone can have such an old man's face, such eyes? And he thinks, yes, what is the matter, what answer can you give to that? I shudder. Or better still, Latin, me shudders, and he says, "Space passed by just now. Outer space." He tries to say it in the most Dutch way possible, in order to make himself sound ridiculous. Otherwise, it would sound too weighty for a first acquaintance. And already fainted once. And

40

already drunk. The old man, a leathery human head with a beard growing from it, comes up to him and shakes his hand lengthily. "*Usted amigo de la señora?* A friend, hah?"

"*Si, si,*" he says, "a friend, a very old friend."

The head nods wisely and slides behind the bar, among the bottles.

"*Qué van a tomar los señores?*"

He says, "A cognac?"

But she goes up to the old man and says "*No, no coñac, está muy borracho ya, el señor!*"

The leathery face gives André a look of sly pity and mutters, "Ts, ts, he drunk. Ha! *Coñac español . . . muy malo para los extranjeros. Hee hee!*"

They drink tepid beer. It gleams dull and yellow on the marble, Cerveza Damm, and he thinks, as if I wouldn't get drunk on that.

"Shall we go?"

Through the little panes in the door, he sees that the group in front of the church has slowly begun to move off and is now turning into a lane that disappears with a sharp bend into an olive orchard, a slow rustic penitential procession that raises small explosions of dust. The tall figure of painter Schramm rises above all others, gesticulating to his lowly disciples, and suddenly André wishes he was walking there, too. How great is the distance? A hundred meters at most, but the silence and the starkly outlined field between him and the group stretch the distance. To go there would be like trying to enter a painting or mingle with the living. Is he the only one who isn't there, then? And he turns again and gazes into the cavern from which they are looking at him, their faces armored with the copper sun, and he says to her he thinks they ought to be going, "otherwise we'll be too far behind." She pays, he reads the latest messages on the brown walls and the food displayed behind the glass, *mejillones en salsa de tomates, nitrato de Noruega, Escuela de Agricultura, curso elemental cada miércoles en Santa Eulalia del Río.*

They take leave elaborately and let Señor Miguel drop back forever into his long rustic afternoon. The great trip has begun.

12

Begun, never to end again. He stands, white, in the light of the classical night, by the open window, facing the sea. A few steps away from him, she turns and groans in the bed. He goes back and looks at her. Her face is distorted into an extreme unfamiliarity, it can never again be that of a woman with whom he has slept. He lifts her head slightly by the tousled hair and very briefly blows into her open mouth and looks from close up at the dark blotches on her face. When he pulls the blankets away from her, she lies naked like a curled-up body without a person in it, a strange and aloof object that could be made of anything. He would be able to destroy it, he thinks with a shudder. Walks to the window and back again.

He strokes the dry skin of her arm, scaly white from the salt of the sea, and thinks, everything will happen now, hatred, fear, it is all about to happen.

Outside, the mad beast he has heard all night starts making its measured sounds again. Glook-one-two-glook-one-two-glook-one-two. Between the sounds, long stretches of night are suspended in which his hatred expands and hangs over her in the hard, crooked bird-of-prey's hand with which he wakes her. She grunts. "Why are you waking me?"

She sits up, an old doll, and pulls the sheet over herself, a mad senator. Suddenly she hears the night, the carefully moving silence, she sees him standing with his hatred, a child-cleric through whom flows an old man, his silhouette stuck photogenically in the moon against the whitewashed wall, the half of his face that is turned toward her an empty plain, the map of Manchuria. This is too bad, she thinks, and asks, "Did we sleep?"

He looks at her, and the empty places fill up with emotions, hurt feelings.

This is how she sees him, weaker than she thought he was, and she thinks of eating, devouring. Her face is burning, her throat is burning, she feels how much she must have drunk. "Will you come to me?" she asks. Oh no, he won't come. For at least a minute, he does not go to her but stands by the window in his magnificent pose, which contains so many sentiments, so still that both of them hear the palm leaves hissing outside, as if they are being fried. Then he goes to her and pulls the sheet off her and bites her until she hits him on the neck and he crawls panting into a corner of the bed against the wooden side.

"What did we do this afternoon?" she asks. One moment you see a man walking around, dragging his life along with him in his belabored face, the next moment he is lying in a corner of your bed, mingling a half hidden chuckle with sobs. Before treatment, after treatment, what kind of machine have we been through this afternoon . . . ?

She gently strokes his skin, with small taps against his ribs. "Did we sleep together?" she whispers.

He looks at her, partly because of that unexpectedly childlike tone, and they see themselves, two beings on their floating bed, alone in a world that has assumed the appearance of a nocturnal bird and says glook outside.

"You wanted me, didn't you?" he says, but that is nonsense. It can never have been enough, it has been done by design: the long journey, the afternoon in the cave, the meal in the *fonda*, the warlike taxi ride back, the dismissal of the previous lover, or was it not like that? He rewinds the day to the afternoon. The walk across the dusty square at San Carlos, with her holding his hand. He was sick in the church and felt ashamed, but now he dances on thin legs behind the group of pilgrims that has vanished behind an olive grove, the same pilgrims he saw from where he was sitting in Miguel's bar, whose soft, luring murmurings he can still hear, and he wants to be with them.

The Spaniard who still belonged to her in Santa Eulalia looks at him with incredulous hatred. And this flatters him, a small reward for the fears and hesitations he has endured, which have gradually become a specialty of his that is not unprofitable, for he is, after all, walking beside her.

The punishment is bound to come, he thinks, and he is right. The punishment has already begun. He holds her hand more firmly, looking like a light-hearted person in summery clothes, a young man, not necessarily the main character of a book, or, as the case may be, of this book.

13

Well, then, repeat the afternoon once more? The net that lifted him up and held him suspended between heaven and earth, a group of lonely scouts to whom the countryman becomes identified with the landscape, to whom all people working on the land stand pinned on the fields as objects, and should he belong to them?

This is no longer the merry drunken frolic of the morning. The sun is too mordant, and they are roaming too forlornly along the narrow hill paths, on both sides of which the landscape drops away. Schramm sings an unintelligible song, and North declaims poems by Shelley in a withering tone. Cyril, who has difficulty keeping up with the group, has cut a branch from a tree and trudges like a flockless shepherd on the compass of their voices. André lags behind, and from time to time they pause and scratch each other with their nails, bite each other in the mouth and say not one word, not one single word to each other. The landscape becomes more barren, here and there a rock juts out of the ground, the true character of the land comes to the surface, the path also becomes steeper, there is less shade from trees. Sometimes the world has dropped so far away that they see the farmers crawl with their oxen over the creased, bloodstained cloths, a battleground of fields.

They rest. The crickets saw holes into the afternoon, and North says, "Do you know what that cricket noise is? Ah! Doesn't anyone know what that cricket noise is? I'll tell you. Inside each cricket there is a tiny black ball, which the cricket thinks is a cricket, perhaps that it is himself. To prize that little ball out of its prehistoric little body is the highest goal of a cricket's life. It saws its way toward itself. An example to us all."

In the silence that follows, they all listen to the sound of the crickets.

44

"Who am I? Who am I?" croons Schramm, and an old German writer, also armed with a cleft shepherd's staff, contorts his Gothic face into the doleful creases of one tormented and says, "Thomas Mann . . . *ich meine,* Thomas Mann . . ." and suddenly falls silent. North goes up to him and strokes his bald skull, then looks at his hand.

She has pulled his face under hers and wets it here and there with her tongue, while two bushes farther the Spaniard watches shyly and timorously. André hears the working of her tongue in his ear, but under it, like a mystical machine, he hears the sound of the crickets incessantly sawing themselves to bits on their way to themselves. A beautiful parable, he thinks, only North could have thought of it. Someone higher up lets a closed bottle with something inside it roll down the hillside, but he moves it along before she has time to pick it up. She hits him for that, but he turns away from her, thinking, I am becoming less, less and less, every experience makes me become less, I see myself wearing away. Is it self-pity that I think this? He closes his eyes and ponders her. Tonight I shall lie in a bed with her and I don't even know which bed. Biting his finger, he asks himself if he desires her, but even that he does not know. It has all happened already; it has to be.

There does not even exist a word for what is happening to me, he thinks. And everything that takes place means only this: that I am becoming less. The human is being pared away from me, the answers to the riddle are wearing off, only the riddle remains, a riddle with no one to solve it, therefore not yet a riddle. Quickly a vague meditation about writing, but then he laughs again at his own thoughts, which mean nothing, not even to him, because they are so indistinct. Moreover, she has put her hand under his shirt and cautiously begins to feel him; this is bound to interrupt his feeble series of images. He listens to the sound, sensuous ants, then buries his head in the lukewarm hollow of his arms in order not to have to see the light and moves forward, very slowly, in the wake of his thoughts. He does not overtake a single one of them, he is unable to think. Floating among his emotions, his anxieties, he tries to disentangle his estrangement, but he drifts into a breathless no-man's-land: I do not exist at all.

He pushes her hand away and says in the tone of a sixteen-year-old at a debating club, "And what purpose do you serve?" She turns round above him and looks into his face, incredulous. "What do you mean?"

He turns away and gives no answer, but she pursues him and then he says, half to himself, "And just imagine what I would have known if I had learned to think."

"What nonsense."

He shakes his head. "No, no."

"Yes, yes. What you mean by that would have been of no use to you. You are an actor. An actor who constantly sees himself, with the landscape and your environment as entourage. You'll never find out anything that way, and when you start thinking about it you even spoil your acting into the bargain."

Irritatedly, as always when someone says something about him, he gets up. It only wanted for her to comment on that, but she says nothing further. She has got up behind him and takes him by the hand and pulls him along with her down the hill, at breakneck speed, and he lets himself be pulled, his legs can't keep pace. Shrieking with laughter, they fall together into a clump of low bushes, where they lie among the branches that painfully begin to rearrange themselves.

"Don't be such a bore," she says. "Tell me your name again."

"André, André." He notices that she doesn't like the name, she flings the word into afternoon, and more decisively than ever he breaks away from himself and hears himself saying his name once again. His name, which he is not, which he is.

At the top of the hill the others have also got up, and together, she already standing, he still lying down, they look at the brass-rimmed silhouettes against the light and with a long *s* the word *queeste* occurs to him. He laughs and says, "It is an old dream of mine to go to the center of Spain, where there are blank spots on the map, emptiness, and to stay there." Softly, and almost giggling, he adds, "In order to suffer."

She opens her mouth to say something but doesn't say it. She turns and starts climbing the hill, panting slightly, and he knows she does it in order to hide her comparative distaste for what he has said, and that is another reason for laughing, but with less conviction. Yet, in the mirror he has held up to himself, it was not insignificant: facial features reminiscent of Saint John of the Cross, intensified by the desolate landscape behind his back, blind white eyes, and on the inside of this, visible only to the owner, the first traces of truths obtained by suffering. Trumpet music. "Hey, Dutchman, hey hey!" shouts the Irishman from above, throwing down a half-full bottle with all his might. André catches it, and she has seen it. Satisfied with himself, he climbs, drinking, toward the others. But is the landscape still useful? No, it has gone bad, it is rotten. I think, I think trouble is brewing, he says to himself, and remembers he has thought a minute ago—last year?—I am becoming the story of a madman.

Looking back, he knows that she can do it as well as the whole of Spain: send him to his emptiness along the spirals of which he is circling. After all, she doesn't need to clarify anything, he already knows that she can do everything she likes with him, even destroy him if she wants to, anybody could, but she has come exactly at the right time, like a train, not by chance, but because he wants it, the dark longing for failure continues to grow inside him, and the disgust that goes with it. He stands still and wants to have an attack. He wants to be so afraid that he may be allowed to scream and yell again, as happens sometimes when he is alone, but now that it has to happen it doesn't happen, he rotates like a doll in his own nonsense, the landscape with those figures in it is thrown over his head like a sack, and the silence of it all fastens itself to him. With effort, as if for the first time, he begins to walk again when the rapture is over.

At the next hilltop, the island is a huge dying person beneath him. He will have to search for its eyes and close them, and so he stands for a long time over the gleaming blind eye of a farmyard well.

"Are you going to jump in?" It is Schramm's voice asking this, a mixture of mockery and concern. Glad that he elicits at least this, he looks up at the painter and asks hopefully, "Do I look like it?"

Schramm throws back his head and whistles scornfully through his teeth. "You look like everything! Do you know what you ought to do?" Educative pause. "Work!"

The word pushes him back to the edge of the chessboard, very briefly. With a pawn's eye, still himself for a moment, he surveys the battlefield. Fallen king, crumbling castle, the horses halfway across the field, and the queen with Clara's face, slightly enlarged, shaking her head at him.

No.

"This afternoon isn't jolly enough?" says Schramm and pushes him away from the well. "Let's go."

Much later in the afternoon, they arrive at San Vicente. He has stopped the circling of his thoughts, has joined in the singing, has caressed her and whispered, in a game of promises (what they will do to each other in the night). It turns in the end into a day for schoolboys, and he is cheerful. Stop thinking, stop thinking. And: I belong. We are on our way to somewhere. And again: I have a woman of my own.

They have arrived by the sea. Above tall cliffs, the dirt track winds along the edge of an abyss, in the abyss the sea is bristly and white, further away it becomes a firmament gathering more and more light, into which they can barely look, and here too, on land, all the colors are crazy and the air trembles. Half an hour later, after a laborious descent, they are lying on a beach of big white round-polished lunar rocks, Cala San Vicente. Straight ahead of them, the water hisses, leaps a little toward them. He inhales the cool salty air as deeply as he can and would like to go for a swim. She lies beside him and gently strokes his arm. "What are you thinking?" She asks again, "What are you thinking?"

"The longest day of my life . . . Not only time, but I myself and the landscape, everything is being elongated, this is the longest day, and at the end of it I shall break. The smallest beginning of breaking."

More romantic talk, she thinks, and with something resembling distaste she withdraws her hand and knows she does not want him more often than once, or for no longer than a week . . .

Perhaps I ought not to embark on this at all—this is the thought that occurs to her as she looks at the long, well-trimmed tips of his fingers. No good for anything, those fingers. She drops a stone on his hand, but the hatred with which he looks at her takes her by surprise.

48

"You shouldn't do that," he says. And then the afternoon suddenly slows down for her, too, and the evening rises more slowly in the hills behind them, swaying its huge body toward the plains of the sea.

Gray, gray, and they get up, ever more forlornly, and walk into the land, a valley now, among the hills, a path, low *fincas*.

Of course the dogs bark. He is now very tired but does not protest when they start climbing again. Schramm has positioned everything strategically, because the entrance to the cave is not indicated anywhere. From below, the hill looks like a closed front of shrubs; Astarte's caves are nowhere to be seen.

Then, loosely scattered about the dark hillside, they crawl toward the top, startling animals with their voices, and slightly apprehensive, as if they were not really allowed to do what they are doing. From time to time, he hears her calling, and he thinks, that is her voice, but he does not call back. North is the first to find the cave, a cold damp hole.

"This is where virgins were sacrificed to Astarte," whispers Cyril. And they try to imagine it, that virgins were sacrificed here to Astarte,and even to feel something like pity, or whatever it is, but the moment is irrecoverable and therefore also the emotion, and the dripping red walls of the cave know nothing about it. He takes a few steps toward the Campari-colored, icy cold walls. The suggestion of blood is obvious, and perhaps this is why he cannot stop himself from touching the tear-stained stone again and again, but his hand does not become red.

"Pray, Schramm, pray!" That's North. And they laugh, but even so, they are startled when the painter's voice leaps up, a strange, high-pitched wail that catches them by the throats. André feels her gripping his hand, for the sound that Schramm utters bounces back from the walls all around, it implores and threatens, but it is much worse than that. Sounds without words, the language in which the painter wails his prayers does not exist; he makes words with long, sick vowels and Slav gutturals, and he dances about in front of them in the light of a small flashlight, jumping before an alcove in the wall, his back toward them, shaking his long thin body back and forth like a gnarled branch until

North grabs him by the waist and pulls him away, shouting, "Stop that, you damn idiot, stop it stop it!" But laughter is the only answer he gets, senseless laughter; the painter rolls over the ground in convulsions and chases North farther and farther away by kicking at him with his legs.

"That's what happens when painters start praying," says Cyril and carefully, holding his stick in front of him like a blind man, he begins the descent, heading for the lights of the *fonda* in the valley below. During that slow journey back, the night draws its veils over the island. Astarte herself helpfully lets her coldest iron shine in the sky.

14

Many hours later. Abundant clouds pass across the sky, almost always without touching the bright light of the moon. The only taxi willing to take them to Santa Eulalia ploughs through the sand of the hill track like a lonely tank in a military campaign. Any moment they may be shot at, or run into an ambush.

She leans drunkenly on his shoulder, her Spaniard, an immobile figure pinned beside the driver, waiting for his tragedy.

He himself is playing a slow war movie before his eyes, bits of an old flickering newsreel, any moment tanks with swastikas will come rolling from the oleander bushes in the dunelike hills, their color a beautiful gray, glamorized by the moonlight, squirting puffs of death that at the first touch will destroy, devour their own kind. He feels he is shrinking slightly, becoming grimmer, better adjusted to the dimensions of a tank, and he aims his forefinger accurately at the Spaniard and shoots him dead.

What a day! His whole life emptied in one day, all that he could call his past, that beautiful amorphous air bubble full of touching stories has aligned and related itself to the events of this day alone and flung him forward onto an open, brightly lit square where she was already present.

"And it isn't even love," he said softly, but this word aroused more laughter, and he had to look at her, at that almost enchanted ugliness so drunk on his shoulder, jolting with the car.

And now I shall even have to go to bed with her. She opened her eyes and saw him thinking it and had to laugh. Pulling herself up by the strap beside the window, she whispered, "This is of no real importance." She said it with great dignity because she knew how hard it would hit him. She had been aware in advance of the suddenly heightened tension in his face, of the breath being sucked in through his teeth.

They entered Santa Eulalia. His eye noted the white square shapes of the houses on either side and saw that they were driving past Marcos' terrace. Later, near the bridge across which he had come to her that afternoon, the taxi took a sharp turn to the right and began to climb a tall hill.

All three of them got out. He paid the taxi driver and turned and looked at the house. It was tall and white and was called Villa Gertrudis. Through an archway between two square columns, crowned by rambling geraniums in tall pots, they entered. The Spaniard tried to slip into the house before she did, with a key, but she slapped his hand away and looked at him for a moment. Again he made a gesture as if to go in, but she slowly shook her head, no, and he took a step back and looked at André.

She made a pointing gesture as if to say *you'd* better see to this, and he felt he was breaking out in a sweat. She had already gone ahead, but halfway down the corridor, her shoes ticking like a clock on the stone floor, he heard her turning back. Of course, he thought, she doesn't want to miss any of it, there might even be a fight, who knows! About her! He scraped his foot across the concrete garden path and said to the Spaniard, "You'd better leave now."

The man looked at him without anger, more in surprise, and then shook his head. He said something to her in Spanish, and when this had no effect either he began to adopt the most magnificent poses: sorrow, despair, one white arm raised to heaven in imploration, a quivering moustache. Oh God, all we want now is tears, thought André, doesn't the fool realize how much enjoyment he is giving her? While the amateur performance continued (you are my whole life, and other fine Spanish phrases), he stepped forward and gave the fellow a shove.

"*Vaya, vaya,*" he said, and the man stopped moving his eyes and looked at him, all the bad nights and all the nonsense and her scorn, and it was as if André were looking into his own face, a head of cotton wool, ready for any sorrow, prepared for any humiliation, oh what a mirror of the future is being presented to me here, he thought, and he hit out at the face with such force that the man toppled back with a howl and remained slumped against the column like a groaning ornament, the night full of sobs and curses. She turned round for the final blow, something like "What kind of officer are you?" or "Well well, these Spanish officers." But André edged past her through the door, still trembling with rage. Washing his hands, he looked out over the moonlit path, scene from my life, Photo SX-1200, composition: she in doorway, shadow of open door cut out into garden path, flanked by two columns. Behind it, blackness, sea, night, the man, pressed against a column, wailing and shouting for his *maletas,* for the money he had given her. Palm trees, rrs, rrrs, and the rustling of long oleander leaves. Go on, write it all down.

He flicked the water from his hands and dried them in his hair, but the blow he had dealt the man had deceived her even less than himself, scorn was already in her eyes, preceded by the cunning with which she tried to conceal the scorn. She pulled him along into a dark room, onto a bed, and started biting and kissing him, but he wrenched himself free and walked to the window.

She came up to him gently and asked what he was looking at. He put a finger to his lips and pointed at the white figure of the Spaniard who, carrying a suitcase and looking back from time to time, disappeared behind a curve in the hill.

"So what?" she said. "So what?"

"That's me," he said. "Me."

She took him by the shoulders and turned him toward her. "But that isn't what I take you for," she said, "that isn't what I take you for." And slowly, as if saddened by what he said, she walked across the room to the light and switched it on.

He sees her, he sees the whole room breaking and shifting in the light, she with her iron face in the corner where the mirror hangs in its wooden frame, the black flag of a dress over it. *The burning writing.* He thinks it and thinks, what does it mean? And all the time that small phrase is crossing his mind, the same sweet Mexican line, *"Aunque a veces la suerte nos pague,"* and the *burning writing.* Moving his foot and at the same time dragging that burning along, the soul of his writer, lying fallow and pale on the grate, curling up like a match stick!

"Though sometimes we are struck by fate." He is now chasing a whole misshapen army of soldiers, loving and kissing themselves in grubby mirrors, into the longest seconds of his life, seconds in which angst lifts him and places him across the boundary where his former, clearer fears came to a halt. Screaming in every hollow of his body, he experiences the worst dizziness; it is not only the world that is breaking away from him now, and the words, but he is breaking away from himself, and again and again the inadequate machine of his language continues (the crazy, childish little machine of his profession), continues to seek comparisons, metaphors. But he can no longer think of anything.

She will come to him, she will not approach him but *appear* to him, he will see her face and she will ask him what is the matter with him, and what is the matter with him? Kicking with his feet for words like a drowning person kicks for firm ground, he receives her, and she sees in his eyes what he is being robbed of, what he is robbing himself of, how he has exchanged the dream for the terror, his child for the corpse he will be, his expectations for the freezing of his expectations. He dies, but it is not enough, she dies, people die, the earth becomes smaller and rolls away, no one has ever heard of this planet, no one has ever existed, for this is what gnaws at his existing body. No one has ever existed. He sees himself shrinking and swelling in the emptiness that is not there, that is there, and with this iron demarcation line between his body and the future death of his body he cannot live. She cannot bear to listen to the wailing, which begins softly, but neither hitting nor caressing, nothing can remove the ashes of his visions from his eyes. Sighing or crying, he turns toward the window and crawls back to the anecdote of his life. The irreparable change, announced a hundred times, has at last occurred. With a moistened white cloth she wipes the wetness away from under his eyes, from around his mouth, the trembling slowly ebbs away, the sick man goes to the bed and copulates with her like a doll, thinking bitterly (this is beginning to function again or has it never stopped?) while he looks at the genuine passion under him—the head turning sideways and sighing, suddenly so weak as if a soft breeze on the beach could have moved it. The calling of his name. She doesn't know it is no longer valid, but the suffering, even that of nameless becoming, it is a healing herb that can be administered. He thinks, I surrender even the last things, and utters, because of the ridiculousness of that thought, a sort of inward chuckle. He wants to read something in her bird-screams, but what?

After this joint plane crash, he keels sideways, neatly, his visor opened toward the square night, thinking simultaneously in his life and in his not-life, and tasting how dangerous this is in the fear that is now no longer not-present anywhere, and thinking perhaps she hasn't even seen it. And suddenly he also hears the sound he must have heard when he stood there, glook-one-two-glook-one-two-glook, of the night-animal outside and the color of the moon and how she did not come to him but he went to her and pulled the sheet away from her, or wasn't it like that? Now, now that he is keeping his eyes averted from the square night and looks at her body and covers it with literary comparisons, her belly is . . . and her breasts . . . as if she . . . Shoulders, the smoothness of her skin, everything gets its turn, and he remembers that she said something about bodies and dying that afternoon, something like we are only our body and when that's gone we are dead, and the space we now occupy will then suddenly be empty. And with superior self-pity he knows how immensely larger and more awesome his fear is, an emptiness that continues to pour into him, insane certainty that no one with ordinary fears will ever take away from him. In that tumbled landscape—desert, fat green decaying Dutch summer, ice floes here and there, bare Spanish mountains—there is suddenly, without any warning, that car driving right through the middle of the land, the car to which he immediately gives a name, the car, the little car of truth: that he wants to die.

"No no no no," he says and starts tossing and turning in the bed, and she sits up and touches him. But he turns away and groans, and plucking at the sheets pulls himself into an upright

54

position. Pushing away, he runs to the window, behind which is the night that could just as well have been serene, and tries to throw up clinging to the window-frame and tries to give himself up, lets his stomach send billows, but nothing happens, no food, drink, no soul leaves his body. In the clearness that then briefly exists, he says, "Theater again. Nothing is so terrible but it still speaks with words," and though his voice, "Fine thing you've brought into the house," perhaps knowing that she will with both hands grab the nurse's role being offered to her. She leads him away from the window, puts him down on the bed, says it will go away, it will go away, dabs water on him, gives him sleeping tablets. He turns and squirms under her hands, and when he has calmed down and before the pills take him away, he finishes the last prayers on the wheel, surprisingly humane in character, in the vein of what have these doings (doings!) of mine to do with what is real and placed in time (what can he mean by that? real illnesses? or concentration camps? the naked and dead?) with the existing suffering of the others—of real people? And then he falls asleep, someone who for the first time has wanted to die.

15

A hesitation, and a preference to remain in that world of shadows. But he washes up on the shore of his sleep and builds himself up from what is nearest: a woman sleeping beside him, bed, floor, the wild wall with the window through which he sees gray olive trees and palm trees and the white, outstretched sky. There you lie, dear friend, and you turn this way and that on your pillow in order to find sleep again in its warmth because you are unwilling. Very cautiously you begin to think. The pain with which his fear of that night returns (not *returns,* with which he *remembers* it) bewilders him briefly, and this bewilderment is both hate and shame. He hates himself and is ashamed because *he* is his fear and he knows it. Nothing overwhelmed or overpowered him, there was not one moment in his life that did not lead to this, there is not one moment in his life that has not contributed to that fear of yesterday.

He sees a packet of Ideales lying beside the bed and lights one. The smell wakes her and she gets up. She is naked, and he turns his head away.

"How are you feeling?" she asks.

"All right."

She comes up to him and kisses him on the eyes. When she bends over him, he feels her breast on his shoulder, and he trembles and clings to her imploringly. She strokes his hair briefly and detaches herself. He gets out of bed and walks to the window. The village lies to the left below him, and he sees the kiosk where they sat the day before. Under the tall tree sits a small group of people, but he does not recognize anyone; they are too far away. The main street, which runs from the square to San Carlos, cuts the village in half. Calle Mayor. Close behind the village begins the green sea, stretching away smoothly and only much farther away fading into the gray of the morning. Small boats. He pulls a few leaves from the olive tree by the window. They are still wet, and he rubs them over his face.

"Does this happen to you often?" She has come up behind him, has kissed him in the neck. He thinks, don't say yes, you mustn't, it is too dangerous, and he thinks, does this happen to me often? Not this, not like this, and he says, "No, never, I think I must have been exhausted," and in the same tone, "I am in love with you." Well, why not? Perhaps it is true. He watches her pensively as she walks out of the room, her *patas* slishing over the stone floor, her dressing gown swaying behind her.

"I am in love with you," he says again, more in general this time, i a o i u, no, i a i o i u!

In the village, a man walks along the main street with a bell and calls, *"Pescado muy fresco y gambaaas, cigalas! Gambaaas."* He thinks, what should I do now? and he wanders, peering curiously, around the moments of his life, perhaps with a certain nostalgia. Each moment forms part of the way in which he is standing here, decorated with a window in a whitewashed house in Santa Eulalia, but is this playing back of the film an explanation of the film? At any rate, it is the film. And then again, the naming that as usual has to take the place of thought.

He in Paris, he sailing in a ship across the ocean and someone standing by him when he scrubs the rusty washroom floor with a pad of steel wool while the sea keeps pushing him against the wall and he feels sick but daren't be sick, he with a black woman in Senegal, he in the intermission at a theater in Leicester Square—as if all theaters, all women, the ocean, Paris, existed only for him, the world a stage, the people extras, and never yet a single actor. Or, he the only and therefore deformed spectator, grown insane from isolation, an eye trying to become a human being. She reenters the room, fully dressed now.

"Are you coming down for coffee?"

He goes to the bed to get his clothes and puts them on. Before they leave the room together, he holds her back. "I want to come and stay here," he says.

Without turning her head or moving her position, she looks at him and says, "That's all right."

As he shuts the door behind him, he hears that it is suddenly starting to rain gently, and when he is walking in the rain it is as if from now on he will be able to suppress all thought of that night's panic. But he knows it isn't true, or perhaps he doesn't even want it to be true. He knows it will come back, and back, until he is destroyed. Whether this is melodramatic, he isn't sure. That thought also makes him shudder.

16

They take a narrow path down the hill. To their left and right, cactuses grown into insane shapes, taller than people. They have no eyes, he thinks, and cautiously bends over in order to pick a small flower from somewhere among the spines. She puts it in her hair, which is already wet with rain, and with an air of gaiety she takes his hand and they walk, talking nonsense, to the kiosk.

Schramm, North, and Cyril are already there and greet them exuberantly. Swaying, North stands up in order to kiss her and says to her, "Did you catch the beautiful white fish? Tender meat, ta-la-la, tender meat, tee-le-lee." She pushes him back into his chair and dips a finger in his glass of rum and wipes it over his spectacles so that for an instant he can see hardly anything and gropes toward André like a muttering doll to shake hands with him.

He notices that Schramm, the only one who is not drinking, watches him with a certain tenseness, and he says, "I'm going to move house to Santa Eulalia."

The painter shrugs his shoulders and says, "So as to work better, I suppose?"

"Work," mutters North, "writing isn't work. Writing is being. That ought to be enough. Any idiot can write. Any damn idiot can . . ." He drops back into a sullen silence from which he bounces up every now and then to ask if they will share a taxi. Each time she says, "No, we'll go on the bus."

"The bus?" Cyril tilts his head sideways so he can look at her even more hungrily. "You cannot possibly take the BUS! Look at that ENORMous quantity of FAHMers, my dear . . . you won't get a seat at ALL! And besides, they all smoke POTA! That will kill the lot of us!" It is making him sick already, and he performs a mime in which he fans clouds of island tobacco away from himself and contorts his face as if unable to bear the suffocating air. "I can't stand POTA. I love them all, but I just cannot stand POTA!

"Do you want to get a taxi?" she asks him.

North interrupts. "Or doesn't old Mr. Peseta approve? It's only thirty pesetas per person."

So they take a taxi. The road, the landscape, are being played back. I drove past here yesterday, and am I still the same person, here and now? Was I less yesterday, or am I less today? No more shouting, the sun has vanished behind the hills, the rain has painted a little more greenness into the landscape, that is all. So many preoccupations!

From several kilometers' distance, they can already see the town, high and white on its hillside between clouds like faded gray cloths. Time running into itself. His first arrival? This is a town of great importance. And he was reluctant to leave the ship!

Curving around the harbor, they enter the town. The drowned ship in the marshy corner. The green a different green. *Otro verde.* Behind the pier, the sea is shaking, its color that of a disinfected swimming pool. He looks at her, tries to see her. Why am I going with her? I should stay here, stay with Schramm, and he repeats in a whining refrain, stay with Schramm, stay with Schramm, but it does not penetrate, or, he thinks, I am looking too hard. You can't look with a knife. With a knife? I mean, he thinks, you cannot peel the body away from the soul. Body and soul, the smell of boarding school.

The taxi deposits them in front of Domingo's. Another endless session begins. "Vicente! Viceeente, *hombre! Dos rons. Y un coñac, eh, Fundador. Ee para mí un Osboshne*"—this is Cyril. She takes an *absynta,* and they raise their glasses to one another, beige, brown, bright green, raise their faces and look at one another, five evil spirits brooding on mischief. But what kind of mischief? They pull at the strings of their endless lives, they open and close like certain marine animals and that is how they sit, two hours, three hours, slow trails of words hang languidly from their mouths in the immense silence of the seabed. The water around them is still, still and invisible like time. Gently, gently, they are pulled this way and that, drifting with the current, still talking, telling stories that they slowly pass to one another.

André swivels a quarter of a turn in his oblong green leaves and peers with his very white face through the invisible water, invisible, church-shaped air in a church, at her, at North who says, "Ecstasy." He hears it clearly, *ecstasy.* Becoming wild, he looks at the ground, at the rock to which he is fixed. He cannot escape. She, at Domingo's table, sees him growing restless and shifting in his chair, she knows he wants to get up, go away. His eyes narrow, and he breathes fast. In a moment, she thinks, he will start shouting, or he will really walk away, what's the matter with the man?

He is stuck on all sides, to disengage himself would mean to die, nothing less, to die . . . And make himself ridiculous, he thinks, which is tantamount to becoming at last a member of what exists. Dark shadows over his head. A whole sardine fleet is sailing overhead, high up, on the boundary. These are his own notes again, he wanted at all costs to pursue this underwater metaphor, which led nowhere, to its final conclusion, and then learn lessons from it with the aid of impossible symbols, everything scribbled down carelessly, in the manner of: sitting at Domingo's, or at any rate sitting there at that moment—indoors because it was raining—to be compared with being under water, and then, life under water unreal, but that was the existing, the surface, the boundary, and above it, real life, in which language was spoken, but in which he would have to die. Then the whole awful set-up was again spoiled by an anecdote: from the sailing of a sardine fleet overhead to the light suddenly being switched on by Domingo. Explanation: sardine fishers also suddenly light their lamps when they are fishing, to lure the sardines. "Foolishly he sat in the sudden light . . ." That is how it must have been, yes. Foolishly he sat in the sudden light.

"*Es muy oscuro fuera,*" said Domingo.

"*Sí, hombre, sí. Demasiado! Lo que faltaba era la luz!*"

"*Es siempre la luz que falta . . .*"

"You are absolutely right, old man. No No, he *is* right." Lecture about prehistoric religions, the goddess of light. "*Mejores no hay!* What, what? Philips is Dutch, isn't it? PHILIPS . . . LUZ! It is their Spanish slogan: *mejores no hay!* No better *luz* ha-ha-ha, the best *luz* is Dutch *luz,* ha-ha-ha! Rembrandt! Hah!" And Cyril gets up, leaning on André's shoulder, blows a kiss toward them with a long trembling hand, and disappears coughing into the rain outside.

Clara also gets up to leave, but now he doesn't want to leave anymore. Ecstasy. He has attached himself to this word of North's. Tilting his head back, he asks himself whether that of yesterday . . . in some way or other . . . had been ecstasy, too, and he is sure it wasn't, because at that moment he was unable to let go of himself. Now if I had been able to *enjoy* my fear . . .

She shakes him by the arm. "Are you coming or staying?"

"I have to collect my suitcases from Schramm's."

She nods and runs her hand through his hair. North sticks out his tongue at him and leaves with her. When he sees her going out the door, a feeling of love suddenly comes over him, mysteriously. He gets up to say something to her, something in connection with last night, something by which he will no longer be the weaker one, but she disappears around the corner, busily talking to North without once looking back, and he miserably withdraws his sudden tenderness and turns to Schramm, who has been observing him all this time.

"I like her very much," he says apologetically.

From his height, the painter gives him a penetrating look, like earlier that day, and says, "You are an idiot, and you know it. The village idiot!"

They take the road across the hill, past the barracks where it smells of urine, as always, and where a few mud-colored soldiers hang about in the doorway, looking at the rain. *Todo por la Patria,* it says over the door. Where the real hill begins, there are puddles everywhere, gold mud clings to their feet, and like two celestial messengers, gold-footed diplomats, they make their way through the cordon of olive trees storming up the hill, crackling and spitting in the wind. Carelessly, they throw gestures and words into the wild holes that stare at them from the rockface, imprisoned behind the bars that form entrances to the catacombs of the ancient Phoenician necropolis. The rain becomes heavier, but through the sound he can hear the sea behind the hill. When at last they reach the top, they pause for a while, and the tormented landscape rolls right up to their feet, eaten into from above by low clouds that bite with wide blackish mouths into the hills and the sea, darkening both. Formentera cannot be seen now, only the Island of Rats, whirling in the gray water like a ship cut loose from its moorings. That is where I would like to be now, he thinks, on that buffeted rock where nobody lives. The sea is wilder there than anywhere else. Fountains of marble are thrown up against the yellowish rocks, the breakers crash and pound against the stone, insane cowboys with whips of water. When they look back they see the town, a white broken heap in a pit of shadows, and he thinks that she must now be somewhere in there, probably drinking or God knows what. Something that has nothing to do with him. She probably isn't even thinking of him. But then Schramm pulls him along, and together they begin the difficult descent. A yellow Egyptian dog yelps at them from under a cactus, a squeaky beggarly whine, and as they pass, the animal leaves its shelter and follows them.

"I'll call you Sucker," Schramm says to the dog as they enter his house. "Beautiful, loam-colored Sucker, Podenca Ibicenca."

The dog places its pointed snout under the painter's knee and begins to squeal in abandonment. "I don't understand Egyptian," Schramm rebukes him and takes the animal to the kitchen where it is fed. When he returns, he says, "It can't do any harm having a holy animal in the house. These dogs don't exist anywhere except on this island. You can't take them away with you because they'll die. They are descended from an Egyptian breed of dogs. A very good background. Life and death . . ." Another unfinished sentence. The dog comes back into the room with downcast eyes and seeks the farthest and lowliest spot to lie down.

"I am going to pack my suitcases," says André.

The painter does not reply. He is standing in front of the painting he started yesterday. André sees he has done something to it since he left. In the middle of the painting, there is a large, roughly torn hole. To the left, the beginning of an *s* is still visible, of the word *sun* that was there. The painter runs his hands over the canvas, sticks an arm through the hole as if to take something out of it, and says, "I shouldn't have done that. You should never try to put a dream, whatever that is, into reality. This is not the hole I dreamed of." He turns to André and says, "The hole I dreamed of was alive. It was an emptiness, something that was not there, something that lived." Grabbing the sides of the hole with both hands, he rips the painting apart with one pull and sings, "There goes the painting, 'Sun,' made by the great painter Schramm, American of Jewish descent, and destroyed by his own hands because he let a dream pervert the reality of his painting." In a mutter, he adds, "Probably the first kaddish for a painting, anyway." And then, aiming the full weight of his mystical, black-outlined face at André, he flings the anathema at him: "For a writer, you carry too many books. For a writer, you do not work enough. You make silly decisions . . . you are far too much afraid. Afraid!" Still not enough: with the Castilian clarity submerged in his Jewish New York accent, *"Tienes miedo tu, hombre!"*

It is like that first occasion when he was attacked in a confessional. Accustomed to the two-way flow of sin and forgiveness, he feels the deadly terror when for once, just for once, the vague black figure, the moonlike face that hangs behind the thick mesh and smells sourly of old man, suddenly lurches forward and hisses accusations, no longer snapping up the sins and swallowing them, nodding dozily, the old white hand already hovering somewhere in the dark to draw an absolving cross in the air, but uttering malevolent accusations, reproaches. The same confusion now as then, for this touches him beyond his vanity, right inside his fear, for now he has been found out, found out and indicted.

He assembles his scattered troops and, fighting against tears, he flees, first to the painting, then out of the house, followed by the painter who worriedly runs after him. They stop and stand opposite each other in the rain, and he lifts his face so that at least his tears will not be seen, or can you tell even in the rain when someone is crying? He feels his nervousness rising from his legs, from his stomach, and he thinks, I don't have my pills with me, oh God what am I to do, and he shouts at the painter, "Don't you understand, you twirp, I don't want to write, I don't want to!"

He hears Schramm shouting back above the wind, "You are a coward, coward." And he thinks, I don't want to because I can't, I see everything but it is not enough, I cannot create, fear and intelligence are not enough, I have no strength . . . We are both splendid now, he suddenly sees. He realizes how loudly they have been shouting, with how much joy. He would like to go on shouting and screaming inarticulately at the hills, at the sea, at the face of the painter who has taken off his wings and is standing before him wet and slender and much thinner than he thought, the whole mad dark sky in his back, raindrops like little glass beads on his tired brown face in which the large black eyes blaze and sparkle, louder than his voice, which has suddenly stopped shouting and all the time, almost imploringly, repeats that one word in every sentence, "Work, you have to work, work."

No, no, thinks André, but the painter's long story unfurls anyway, the day when he was walking on Jones Beach (he was walking on Jones Beach and André sees him walking, in cheerful American swimming shorts, El Greco in America, bouncy and waving on the beach, which is, of course, deserted) and there was no one on the beach. "I'd been walking for half an hour, and I stopped and looked back. Behind me, for at least half a mile back, I saw a long trail of footsteps. My footsteps. They could not be anyone else's because it was very early in the morning. White light, American light. The sky squirted all over with morning neon. Only the sea, in the distance, brushed with lobster-colored paint. The day. I placed my foot into one of the footsteps, and it fitted. But at that moment, I saw that the sea—the tide was coming in—took a slow draft and poured it out over the whole trail at once. I had not been there. I had not walked there, no one had been there." Now the moral, thought André, the moral, but nothing came. Somewhere the sun struck a hand of cold brass through the clouds, and the two men were for a few moments illuminated as falsely and unnaturally as in a poem by Góngora, the painter still droning on about work, his impossible parable already forgotten, work, the only thing, and he, André, had to work, that would save him.

"All right, all right," he said. And then, with weary malice, "Sing it like Wagner! Sing it like Wagner! Trumpets! Arbeiten sollst du! Sollst! Sollst!" And with a quick movement, while singing, he leaps up and gives the painter a kiss. Before the moment has melted, he disappears past the inhospitable painting toward the hills where the rain is still at work.

17

His second walk to the hills. The *sollst, sollst* still echoes in his head, and the gusts of rain lashing his face don't help. As usual, he sees himself walking: clubfeet of mud, singing and praying, an excited company of Valkyries and heroes with horned metal helmets and flaxen hair, choirs singing all around him. Wagner! But no, no, the need for clarity is stronger, and he remains alone, the drenched walker from the past, attracted by the rain, lured as others are by a full moon. Whenever it rained like this, he had to go out, walk in it, let himself get wet until his clothes clung to him like a soaked second skin, a failed attempt at comfort and chastisement at the same time, to which he heroically attached a sort of *exercitio* . . . wetter and still wetter he had to be, until . . . Until what?

Once again, something becomes clearer to him as, with a half-ecstatic smile, he walks through the red, shifting fields into the hills, leaving low white farmhouses behind him under gusts of wind, not even noticing the religious swaying of the olive trees that, with wide open branches, see secret things in the clouds. No, nothing becomes clearer to him; he laces himself ever more tightly, blocking every access with his memories. He ruminates on his life, his forest walks, his love fantasies, spurred by an orgy of corroding coldness licking at him. Nothing, nothing has changed. To the person he knows himself to be, nothing has changed, and he wants to go on doggedly identifying himself with that person, the outside of someone he still resembles, who is drifting away from him in time but whom he wants to preserve, and that is why he goes on breaking. But knows nothing, nothing. He has also forgotten his fear in the euphoric, easy mood he decides to regard as ecstasy, in which he can think of her as in a romantic story in which she does not have to become more clearly defined. Forgetting—denying—his wailing and howling of last night, in which the breach had at last become visible. Even sleeping with her can be acknowledged, it is an experience, and does he not need that? Oh God, even writing is now getting mixed up with it, and as he walks on, squelching in the mud, sometimes jumping from stone to stone and balancing on sheep walls, the smile not to be beaten from his face, he sees all the things he is going to do, *do*. From time to time, he recovers himself, calls out aloud, "No, that is too crazy," addresses himself as "boy"—"You can't do that, boy"—or "keep calm." And then he stays calm for a while, seeming, to the humble peasant passing by with his devilish goats and heavenly sheep an *extranjero muy especial*, his hair plastered to his head from the rain, eyes burning, and the ultra-amiable mouth greeting, *buenas tardes!* What on earth can a man like that be doing in the hills? This path doesn't lead anywhere! But it is Saint John of the Cross who goes there, his American windbreaker flapping about him in the same folds in which it will be displayed forever in village basilicas, with fewer candles than the others, not a popular saint.

The narrow trousers cling to his legs, sometimes he hides behind a tree to light a cigarette. He sees a peasant, enwraps him in his romantic vision: peasant, landscape, Mediterranean Sea. Those are people who *really* live, and he does not know that every millimeter he removes himself farther from his own reality becomes mortally dangerous.

And what does that mean? But how else could it be expressed? There he goes, again so high up that he can see the sea over which the clouds ride, low and clawing. The land slides down from the hills in all kinds of paintings, all the way to the high town in which she, Clara, must be. With North. He longs for her. That which he thinks he is, longs for her, imagines something, wants to stay with her, will not be afraid again . . . all the impossible things.

He lies down on the wet ground, strokes the grass around him, thinks, my witnesses, gets up again and walks back along the same path to the town, to Domingo's. She is not there. Only Nescafé Jack sits like a rockface behind his glass of coffee and beckons him to sit down.

"You have been walking in the rain!" There is no need for him to reply to this. But America has more than one string to his bow. "They tell me you're a poet. Are you a poet?"

"*Sí, sí.*"

"What kind of poetry do you write?"

The poet feels his Wagner slipping away. She is not there! He looks around for an anchorage, brown walls, nothing, *calendario,* nothing, *hoy es el día 7 de Febrero* . . . With shame he says, "A lot about death," and hears how ridiculous it sounds.

"Death?"

"Yes."

"Hm." The entire body, transported from Los Angeles, sends auxiliary troops to the brain, which directs the forceful blue eyes once more to the disheveled, drenched boy on the other side of the table.

"You really think that is a subject? Death? You like it? Hah, is that it? Kind of decadent poetry?"

"No, no." He beckons Vicente from his dark corner. "*Un vaporete . . . es coñac caliente, no . . . ?*"

"*Sí, hombre!*"

"*Bien, dáme un vaporete de Fundador . . .*"

The rock advances closer to the table. "I am a poet myself! You want to read my stuff? I was a taxi driver in L.A. Used to write long poems while waiting, you see. I had a volume printed. You know what it was called? *Taxi No. 38476.* I'll give it to you . . ." Behind the bar, the gurgling and slurping of the Gaggia with which Vicente is heating up the brandy. "Let's go to my place, what's your name again, Andrew? Let's go to my place, I . . ." No, no, he doesn't want to go to his place, he is looking for Clara, has Jack seen Clara? "Yes, she was here with Philip North, and Cyril . . . they all went to Pedro's Bar . . ." He tries to remember where that is. "Near Schramm's place, this side of the hill."

The wind chases after him, down the street. Now he will see her again. Hurrying close to the houses where it is dry, he revolves the words of the rock of Los Angeles in his mind. What was it that excited him so much? He draws the two red lines from Los Angeles and Amsterdam to the island and listens once again to their futile conversation—You a poet? Yes yes, I a poet. He a poet. Everybody a poet about death waiting for a taxi—this feeble flowing together of messages that are not intended to arrive, the sliding past each other with words that do not have any strength, and almost fretfully he thinks, why doesn't the fellow say something really crazy?

And then he compares his own Germanic state of mind with the platitudes he has meted out to the American; he sees his inner mind (notes!) as a wild, dangerous world of swamps and "ambivalent illumined grottoes enveloped by a jellyfish-like substance; that which is for the others / the jelly, the untouchable exterior, that which says nothing, an announcement that communicates nothing and commits to nothing. But why this mysteriousness, this masquerade about simple truths? To safeguard the little that he is? (!) [This exclamation mark is not included within the quotation marks employed by me. There is no question of irony in these notes of his. Poor A.S.] Not to be exposed to destruction?"

And then the images that, as always, wash over one's thinking: he observes himself as he walks there, where he is walking now at the end of the Vara del Rey, at the fork of three roads: the muddy track upward to the barracks and the town walls, the road to San

Antonio that curves to the right in a wild sweep, and the third road, the one he has to take, the one to San José.

The wind has free play here and chases the rain in crazy billows over the exposed crossroad and against the little guardhouse where an old man warms himself by a glowing brazier, black-painted Charon himself waiting for his ferry, looking at him with friendly beady eyes that see a passerby and not the mollusk-like glassy layer around him, the man who cannot defend himself in the dead slime that envelops him. Here comes the beachcomber, pushing with his foot against the jellyfish so that the tough clump of glass is lifted and falls back, dragging the invisible writer inside it back to the sea. No doubt he will soon be washed up again.

Now where was I? he thinks, what was I thinking? But he has already vanished between the houses, for the second time that day past the sour smell of the lower barrack, Charon's good-day greeting as a protection in his back, past the Centro Cultural, the Alianza Francesca—"They even have Butor up there"—to where he can already hear the singing. At Pedro's Bar, he swings the bead curtain aside and stands teetering on the doorstep, seen by no one. He enters.

The past of an entire week stands clustered around an old lady who is shaving an old fisherman with an electric razor. He adds up the past as if to try to make bygone time into an object, a fetish, solidified time, with which to observe the invisible change, the changing of his life . . . Cyril whom he met on the boat, North, Schramm, the trip to the cave at San Vicente, all those slow events, Schramm in the regal conversation on the terrace that morning, so long ago already, hours! And she, whom he has known for years, one night, his fear.

Does the fetish work? He feels how he is becoming taut and pale, his skin is actually tightening across his face, he wants to rub it, at least calm the *skin,* but he knows that in less than a minute he will be trembling, will no longer be able to talk, will be in a panic. He pushes the knuckles of his left hand between his teeth and hisses inside the gagged mouth, I don't want to I don't want to, but the terrible merry-go-round is already in motion again, death, nothingness, I want to be dead, I don't want to be afraid, the images of terror tumble about in a froth. And of course now she is coming toward him because she has finally noticed him . . .

Again, again, she thinks, the man is mad, he is really mad— it's too awful to watch, that contorted face, that animal grimace . . . fff, *der junge Werther*. She fetches him a glass of brandy and he drinks it.

"Are you coming?" he asks.

"Where to?"

"I don't know, anywhere. Away from here, at any rate."

"Has it come back?" she asks. The directness of the question hits him; she sees hate flaring up in his eyes, but he is really too far gone and sly enough with it, he needs her now, so he asks her once more to come with him. But again she says no.

At that moment North joins them and puts his hand on his shoulder and says in Cyril's voice, "How is my very interesting Dutch writer doing?"

In the advertising mirror, André sees his face filling up with self-importance, and he even says something in return, lets himself, *cortège*, be escorted to the old lady who, leaning on Cyril's arm, is still busy shaving the old fisherman, a brother of Charon. Zaron, or Paron, or whatever his name is, undergoes it with timid pleasure.

"This saves him five pesetas at the *barbería*," Cyril whispers in his ear. "She is really trimming the old dog, HAH HAH HAH."

The light rains down and falls apart into separate paintings: Pedro Delacroix behind the bar, Cyril Daumier indefatigably supporting old Mrs. Goya, who now, with thumb and forefinger of her left hand, picks up the leathery folds of the fisherman's neck and pulls them straight, the better to shave them, and poor Paron or Zaron Goya, who undergoes it ever more timidly, gently teased by a group of fishermen in a dark corner of the café, badly restored popular painter from the late nineteenth century, while she whom he seeks all the time has retreated to the espresso machine, her hand under the aluminum ridges close to the sulphur-green-shiny-nameplate, Gaggia, with her face shifting back and forth between classical clarity, hideous Ingres, and huge deformities. Clara, he thinks, Clara, and he gradually thinks nothing, not a single coor-

dinated thought, nothing fits, everything breaks, hangs inarticulately in the half-empty, half-finished streets of my emotions,
an English suburb on Sunday. The buzzing of the razor that, from
the moment he entered, seemed to belong to this bar suddenly
stops—the engines of the plane have stalled, they slide down in a
slow, silenced fear.

"Ever met you before?" A cultured voice. The sharply chiseled
face, at once bronzed and ravaged, daily combat between sea air
and alcohol and moreover beautifully made up, looks at him im-
periously. Eyes of iron.

"No, no, I . . ."

But Cyril takes over from him and he hears Poet, Dutch, and
the military face opposite him becomes pointed and says, "You
look like a very sick man, Mister Steen Camp."

. . . Clara's friend . . .

"Ah, Clara, come here, my dear, my love. I told your friend he
looks like a very sick man, uh, like a corpse with fever!" Feevah!

André looks at Clara. What will she say now? This interest
shown in him, the honorific title, must surely enhance his status, it
must have made an impression on her . . . But North cuts through
it in his sharpest voice and says, "He looks like the Pope of Rome
with an idiot inside him!"

Twenty Mexican dogs burst out laughing, but before André
has time to pity himself the old lady takes him by the hand and
says, "You must meet my husband," and pulls him along to a pink
man who sits alone at a table. Blue, totally empty eyes look at him.
He sits down thinking, this man is there even less than I am, and
something in that thought arouses an immense hilarity in him.
The conversation is a flawless copy of Somerset Maugham, the
man who has served somewhere in the tropics makes observations, interrupted at regular intervals for a sip of absinthe. The
woman has left, and when ten minutes later André gets up, a
whole life has been related to him, couched in soft, polished English sentences. He can get up noiselessly and go away, a life of
seventy years drunk up in ten minutes, youth, military career,
future plans . . .

What now? He looks at the chattering crowd and listens to the unbelievable noise. She is standing among the moving people, a stranger, fairly still, and does not look at him. He wants to go to her, but there are immense distances between them. He notes the time on the cheap metal clock above the bar. Fourteen minutes past two. Fourteen hours fourteen, the train departs from the empty man to Clara by the espresso machine. The landscape is endless. The first few days, nothing but crates of Cerveza Damm / Cerveza Damm, Cerveza Damm / Cerveza Damm—there's a nice beat to that. Then worlds of tables and chairs, everything made of wood, the tables rimmed with dull metal, the wood unpainted, marked with damp rings. And the tiles along the wall! While the traveler sleeps, the train passes rock faces of gleaming white tiles halfway up the wall, followed by an earth-layer of dark green ones. The wall above is imitation marble, gray, a badly charted polar region that arouses revulsion. The train stops by the corner of the bar. Long, ribbed strips of wood run diagonally to an underworld of dirty shrimp heads and toothpicks around the red rubber ferrules on the legs of the bar stools, a continent into which huge unhuman feet sometimes stray after slipping from the long, scratched nickel footrest running from one end of the bar to the other.

"No se siente bien, Señor? No se encuentra bien?"

"Ah sí! Bastante bien!"

But the fly's head opposite him will not go away, it wants to dissolve together with his shadow in the beige plastic of the bar, round eyes burn in it, worried eyes that want to brush the hair out of his eyes, wash his face with cold water, and much else.

My timetable, he thinks, my timetable, and peers at Clara sitting light-years away, nearer and nearer to the bead curtain. The hours he will still have to travel . . .

"You feel no good? No good?"

"Sí, sí . . . Dáme un poquito de agua . . ."

"Agua mineral? Vichy Catalan? Vichy quiere?"

Everything shrinks and expands. The fly has vanished buzzingly, slams a refrigerator, returns with a large green bottle from which he pours into a glass. Everything shrinks and expands. The corner of the bar is now so far away . . . the floor is curved. How long ago did Pedro give him that water? Pedro the fly. Once upon a time, he was given water by Pedro. Vichy. He drains the glass. Fourteen sixteen.

"*Gracias, Pedro!*" His voice, rolling out of a megaphone, now reaches his own ears.

"*De nada, Señor! Servidor!*"

Everything is . . . North is standing before him, between the rails. "I'll crush him."

"What's the matter, are you ill?" He is being asked this question a thousand times a day. A plot!

"No no no," he says but obediently allows himself to be led outside, the gravely sick man, oh, past her who sits averted on her stool, still someone whom he does not know. "I wouldn't even be able to describe her."

"Why are you taking me outside?" he asks North.

"Because your nose is bleeding."

Only now does he taste the tepid blood in his mouth. He raises his hot face to the rain. No more shrinking and expanding world . . . "Don't be a goddam neurotic." This he clearly hears North say, and "Why don't you say what's the matter with you?"

The matter. He turns to the hunched American, Trotsky reborn, and says, "Nothing is the matter."

Or does he say, "I am going wild with my poor wild brain scattered all over the place, can't you see I am all over the place, thousands of branch offices everywhere in time busy getting worn out, from fear, I am only here now to dispense comparisons, haul in words, I . . ." But no, he really hasn't said anything. "Idiot inside you." Does North say this now, or has he said it before? "Idiot inside me." But the lucid man of letters who is keeping watch inside him, vigilant little fellow, holds him in check, his fear is saturated with words, a natural phenomenon. As soon as North has disappeared with a shrug behind the rattling bead curtain, he begins to calm down, his head pressed against the wet trunk of a spindly tree on the terrace. If this is the price for writing, I don't want to write. Never before has he known something with such certainty. He takes a deep breath and wipes the blood away with a handkerchief that he has held out to wet in the rain. He does not look at it. A young girl with long blonde hair passes by and looks curiously at him. He looks back as straight as possible and says between his teeth, "Come to me then, come to me then, watch out, I'll get you." Aloud, he says, *"Buenas tardes, muchacha."*

"Buenas tardes."

"I want you," he whispers, following her slender, half-dancing figure with his eyes. "I want to touch you and be healed." With his thumbnail he picks at a piece of the wet bark, which, looked at closely, appears diseased and uneven, a grey and white, shiny, pimply skin. That terrible feeling of contamination, of disease, will not leave him. Mocking himself, yet full of voracity, he starts to run after the girl, knowing that he will not dare say anything to her, that he will not dare touch her. Slowly and suddenly, without mockery, he says aloud to himself, "He pressed a burning kiss on her cool mouth." She enters a house somewhere, and he turns and walks back in the direction of the café. Briefly he hears all their voices, then he has already gone past, on the road to San José. Somewhere to the left must be the path to Schramm's house. What is he to do? Wretchedly torn between a desperate desire to destroy something, stab, cut to death, bite, and to lie howling in a corner, to be stroked and rubbed with the cheapest Spanish perfume, or something like that . . . No. But what is he afraid of? Briefly, in the cool driving rain, on an open stretch of the road, he can truly ask himself that question. Or is the only thing he wants not to be afraid anymore? He remembers the girl's face and looks back with longing.

In the distance, a funeral procession approaches. Whistling softly, he hoists himself up on a sheep wall built of big rough stones and watches the cortège. At the head, a slovenly yokelish acolyte holds a meter-high gleaming black pole with a gray-painted iron crucifix. The wet Christ dances listlessly above the mourners in the rain, a Gregorian waltz. The priest is flanked by two small altar boys in poppy-red chasubles, and peers at the ground mumbling prayers:

> Judex ergo cum sedebit
> Quidquid latet, apparebit
> Nil inietum remanebit.
>
> Quid sum miser tunc dicturus
> Quem patronum rogatorus
> Cum vix justus sit securus.

André whispers the words softly, thinking, now I am cheerful again, now I am cheerful again! He wants to stand up when the bier passes him, but a loose stone falls with a thud from the little wall and everyone looks at him, the priest with a face from which the Latin continues to pour, a face that hates and disdains the pagan foreigners on the island. Oh, he thinks, now to jump among them and call out I want to be buried too, bury me too! High up on the driving box sits an incredibly filthy man whose bony gravedigger's hands hold the reins of an old horse disguised under a black cloth and silver blinkers. The bier must be very old, it squeaks with relish and the coffin sways gently and merrily. There is no doubt but the corpse is laughing.

Behind the bier, on which four tall glass kerosene lamps are burning, walk the mourners. Grief is here hierarchically arranged. In the first four rows, black and broken people, their hard island faces steeped in sorrow. Behind them, a gradual trailing off to the last rows: young fellows with their hands in their pockets and cigarettes between their prattling lips. They have long since forgotten the dead person and laugh and look back at the stranger in the crazy coat who has begun to follow them at a distance of about fifty meters. Lisping like a huge reptile, the cortège turns into a sandy sidetrack, and he continues to follow until they arrive at the cemetery. No one takes any further notice of him; other things require attention now: holy water swishes against the coffin, the laughing corpse is lowered into the earth. An agitated self-pity takes possession of him, for is he not himself being buried there? He, always he. A little warily, he wanders past the open cemetery walls, reads names, José María Tur y Vicenz, Pedro Hermano Marau, María Dols Nogueira. Sometimes he runs his hand over a tombstone and thinks of the perished or half-perished bodies lying underneath, a compact mass of decay, how many there are, and he feels how the same agitation as always sweeps through him, a procession of delusions. He would like to be able to define this blend of fear and attraction but knows he is much too confused at this moment, and every second he stays here, among these seductive dead, it gets worse. He watches as the mourners bend once more with ineffable longing over the coffin as it descends lopsidedly, one more time they bow in the direction of the open ground and scoop up handfuls of earth and throw it after the dead person, and then they turn away, their faces contorted, into the rain, in the moving air.

The priest breathes his eternal comfort over the body, and André pushes farther to the front; he wants to take part in the Latin formulas that he too can whisper, share in their blessing. The total confusion that has shattered his life has suddenly, fleetingly, become visible to him as a wound, and he thinks, I want something on it, balm, magic charms, let someone else just for once take over this pity that I feel for myself. The group around the hole in the ground now responds with slow words to the prayers said by the priest, and some are weeping, water springs from the rocklike faces of the relatives. He sees them and is envious of their abandonment, and again the delusions get the better of him; he no longer believes in this too-visible grief, in mourning. This is a tremendous celebration, a lustful wallowing in the secrets of life and death. Births and wasting diseases fade in pairs, and so do the mysterious actions of killing or dying. Whistling and plunged in the gleaming tar of mourning, the living rise to undreamed-of heights and glide monolithically, like a black barge, past the cypresses out of the yellowish cemetery where he alone remains watching, the seething water behind their propeller abates and lies down. Like a dog, he alone remains, he and the gravedigger, that warmed-up skeleton in a moldy, braid-trimmed black coat shuffling toward the voluptuously open grave, longing in his eyes, a silver spade between his horned feet digging up earth and throwing it on the cheap wood, making the dead body ever warmer. There's a different priest for you! All the engines of the coffin are already beginning to throb! *Vroum vroum,* and the other graves burst open, too. The Yorick priest shoots the universe to bits with a Bengal pistol until the grubby underside of time becomes visible and the first coffins roar past the ragged cemetery walls. The oldest dead are at the front, but it all happens so fast that he can see hardly anything except a whirling suction—the figures on the half-perished coffins are no longer distinguishable, the flapping corpses inside them are clutching their crucifix-wheels tightly, softened bones and slabs of rotting flesh are flying around, and the entire cemetery becomes a whizzing, spinning top whose turbulent air waves brush past him and chase him away, him, the living, existing corpse, the killjoy.

Afire with agitation and shame, he walks in the opposite direction, toward the sea, the land pushing him through orchards of immobile fig trees and among low, smouldering fires, down an ever-more-steeply dropping path to the safe lapping and sighing of the sea, by which he, exhausted and still confused by the sense of well-being he feels in his body, lets himself fall down on the rocky beach. He has an overpowering desire to swim so as to feel himself totally surrounded at least by *something*, and also to take part in a conspiracy . . . But when he notices that he is crying, he hurriedly gets up and goes to Schramm's house. It is still raining. To his right, a few hundred meters into the sea, the Island of Rats creeps through the water. He wonders whether it was really only that morning he was looking at it from Schramm's balcony. If that is so, every hour must be at least a year, a year that pulls him further toward a hidden, above all terrifying, future. And for how long has he forgotten to think of her? This thought makes him pause for a moment . . . that she means nothing in his life, as little as anyone. "I don't know any people," he says aloud and feels that the thought pleases him. Proud of this so clearly formulated, interesting loneliness, he continues his way down the muddy path, avoiding the puddles as best he can.

18

On the wall of Schramm's house a note: "André, we are at Mrs. Cameron's, next door but one. Clara." She has thought of him!

He goes to the house and rings the bell. Howling and yelling of dogs. He hears the voice of the old English lady, "Hush, hush, my dears, hush, come on now, let's be quiet . . ."

An igloo with a sketch of Churchill, brass Turkish pots, a carpet, the first he has seen on the island. Four or five screaming Pekinese leap up at him, trying to bite him. The woman pushes them away but picks up the largest one and holds it close to his face. Out of two slimy balls the animal peers at him, its old face surrounded by a frayed wreath of long hair, a dwarf dressed up as a dog. She tells him the dog is blind, but he does not believe her, sees how the animal is looking at him, the Mongol head sniffing at his soul and rejecting him with a grunt. He isn't even sure whether she is perhaps testing him, but he daren't ask. Slowly and carefully, the monster is set onto the marble again. Mrs. Cameron puts her thin brown hand with the blue lacquered nails on his shoulder, and together they walk into the house. Growling, the dog keeps circling around them, and she gently pushes it aside with her foot.

"Do you like the dog?" The iron blue eyes pose the problem very simply. Mrs. Cameron's father was a general, as is evident from a much-decorated portrait in the hall.

"I don't think so."

"He is very famous. And he's got a very beautiful name. Ching Hei–Tobruk–League of Nations . . . Do you like the name?"

"Yes, I think it's a beautiful name."

"Fine, fine . . ."

Ching Hei–Tobruk–League of Nations follows the fascinating dialogue between his military mistress and the stranger with mistrust and, still growling angrily, walks behind André into the living room.

An empty man is sitting by the window and looking at the sea. Schramm sits crouched beside an armchair, humming softly, and does not look up when he enters. Clara sits with her arm around North, and he registers how much North and the Pekinese resemble each other. The animal nudges the settee with his nervous, long-haired sensors, and North pulls him up by the scruff.

Mr. Cameron rises from his emptiness to bring André a glass of absinthe and speak to him and then disappears again to his watch post, four up four down. His wife is telling an anecdote about Brazil, how dreadfully they were bamboozled there, and what happened then, and he sees how Clara makes a gesture for him to come and sit beside her, and amid Portuguese invective that belongs to the story and Schramm's penetrating crooning he goes to the settee. Clara kisses him on the neck and puts her cold hand up his back.

"Shall we go?" she asks, and he wants to get up, but they stay where they are, a fatal anesthesia pressing them to their seats, for this has to be, never before has the suffocation of being with others oppressed him as much as now. The slow submersion of the afternoon sets in, the atmosphere becomes ever more dangerous, emptier, the woman is still telling her story, nobody is listening anymore except the dogs, behind the window black shadows appear, Schramm lies as if dead beside his chair, with closed eyes, North whispers phrases to the droopy face of the dog lying on his lap.

He passes his hands over her body, her shoulders, her breasts, she slumps further toward him and says something into his ear that he does not understand, does not want to understand, and they turn their faces to each other and look at each other, and he knows she will be able to read every weakness, every hesitation toward her on his face. But she does not want to see anything; with pursed lips, she bends forward and kisses his eyes and his mouth with a tenderness that alarms him more than anything else. He wants to kiss her back, but each time he tries she pushes him away. She holds his neck firmly and turns his face this way and that in the dim gray light, all the time seeking the weakest places in the face that she has ceased to regard as the face of a husband or a lover but which attracts her nevertheless— and not, she thinks, only because of the suffering, as he called it to her, but rather because of the calculated innocence with which he manipulates the age, decadence, and coquettish grief that are revealed in his face. She feels that he wants to retreat, go back, not be discovered, because the discovery is bound to demonstrate the impossibility of a relationship, but at the same time he allows himself to be lured by her hands, the one on his neck that commands him to stay, the other caressing him and seeking him where he is at his most vulnerable, at his most childish. She knows she can make him defenseless, but also that afterward she will hold him in contempt. Whether she is willing to pay that price she is not yet sure, and she decides to wait and see whether perhaps he will still take the initiative, prevail over her.

Mrs. Cameron has got up and gone to her room with one of the dogs. They hear her talking to the animal and see her husband get up against the last light that hangs on the windowpanes. Slowly he comes toward the settee and stands over them and says, "All I ever do is buy food for the goddam animals and feed the goddam animals and sit here and look at that goddam sea," and he totters away again, groping for his chair, while the black patches above the sea grow into a full-scale disease.

Everything is now tainted. North has got up from the settee and lies down beside Schramm, who may even be asleep, and as they listen to the beginning of an endless description of the room they withdraw to their own territory, the tens of kilometers of settee that have become free, where she hunts for him in the plush steppes, with all the time North's voice circling above the warm darkness of their now-closed eyes, the voice that reads the house as druids read the omens. "I see a wall beautiful white but cracked, I see a ceiling white full of meaningful cracks, I see a brass lamp in the shape of the crown of a tree, there are five little lamps in it, the biggest is at the top in the middle of what must have been the top of the brass trunk out of which come the four side branches each with eight leaves of slightly blackened brass each of these has a lamp in it." But while the voice completes the inventory and the empty man is admitted to heaven and Schramm is eaten alive by the Mongolian monster, she beckons him with one finger on her lips to another room where he kisses and embraces her and lies down on the floor with her and he sees her face, which is as big as his, and they roll among the mighty furniture and he takes her, out of love . . .

"Shall we go to Santa Eulalia?" she whispers. "Let's go to my house. I am sick of all these people."

He sits up beside her and caresses her face, a deed. She looks at him wonderingly and does not even know whether she really wants to take him home with her, or whether she wouldn't prefer him to go away now, vanish from her life with that face behind which thousands of thoughts revolve that she will never know about—and such terrible thoughts, she suspects. But he begins to pull her to her feet, and when she is standing he embraces her again and yet it is more like imploring and begging than anything else. She wants to push him away gently, but he clasps his hands behind her neck and strokes her until the tapping of the blind dog's nails on the marble distracts them and pulls them apart.

In the dark, they walk into the corridor, and he feels the dog against his legs and gives him a kick. The animal's high-pitched squeal rolls back and forth between the walls. North suddenly appears in the corridor, reeling drunkenly. He grabs her by the collar of her coat and asks, "Was that nice?" Letting her go, he pushes André against the wall with a bang and says, "Coward, a blind dog! What are you two up to? I want to know . . . I must know . . . I must . . ."

They push him away and go outside, but he follows them, screaming as he overtakes them and, a little way ahead of them, starts to walk backward, slightly floating. It is clear he is walking on air, the same air in which his terrible face hangs, all the blackness of the night around it.

Out of a dark tunnel a taxi draws up. They get in. She opens her arms and he falls into them, away, into a deep sleep from which he awakens a few minutes later. They are on the road to Santa Eulalia. In the light of an oncoming car, he sees her face, and he is filled with wonder. The pain of a sudden, embittered dependence creeps into his teeth, and in order to take revenge he lets his head sink into her lap and pulls her coat over himself so that the driver won't see that he is putting his head under her skirt. As he starts biting her, he hears, through her belly, her body speaking Spanish to the man at the wheel. His mouth gagged by her skirt, he falls asleep again, her presence above him, her image on his retina, her drowned face peerless, its sternness stiff with contempt.

He wakes in the first gray light of morning. Screeching of birds. "I am dying," he hears himself saying. Perhaps he has been saying it for hours. Shuddering, his eyes lag behind the action of a thought: that he wants to murder her. Time and again, his eyes sneak away from her face in the gray light. But the counting continues, and the eyes count her, the blind eyes curtained with sleep, the small purple areas close by, the broad road of her forehead on which the wrinkles move restlessly, the relaxed cheek that runs all the way to a mouth curved in disdain. His hands see it, too, and his fingers hover above the skin of her throat. This is the terrible temptation. He knows he will never do it, will never let his hand fall on that throat and press, but he is so overcome by fear of himself that, slowly and cautiously, so as not to wake her, he gets up and slips away from her. He hides the scissors on the table under a piece of cloth. The nail scissors also, and one by one he puts away the knives where he won't be able to see them, but their presence continues to stab and carve, piercing and tearing a soft substance. Breathless, he runs away from her image, that sleeping doll, and goes to the bathroom, where he sees himself becoming brighter in the new light. Brighter, but not calmer.

He puts his eyes against those eyes in the mirror, but they are not flesh and blood, he does not really have anything to do with that whining, death-obsessed man. He feels his heart thumping throughout his body, the alcohol pressing against his throat, against his stomach. Without much conviction, he begins to throw up, and ten minutes later he stands panting in the doorway looking out, drinking as much air as possible, as if that would let him live forever. He looks round when something makes a soft sound behind him. She stands there watching him. He wants to say hello to her but cannot speak. Her face is barred and refuses him. In the immense silence, his breathing is more terrible than the trees outside. Going toward her—

Now, what chirruping, what shouting. The circle closes, the thousands scream, scream. The man turns in the circle, where the sun is, the gold on his clothing moves. Melting with gold, he walks to the center. The sound of the trumpets has broken. He looks into the hole, the mouth of the *toril*. Silence dawns like a day. Blind with darkness, the bull runs out into the light—

he stretches out his hands toward her, to her breasts. He holds her there and feels her hatred. He stands tottering until she frees herself and pushes him away. He says nothing, does not understand her. The prelude to disaster. Biting his lips, he seeks support from a shadow. She can no longer bear—

With a flashing movement he swings his *capa* into the air. The voices of the thousands vanish, they are absolutely not there. In that gap, he swings the purple glitter far to his right. The bull turns away. The shouting blends with the light. The man changes and becomes a kneeling man. His face does not adjust to the change, it remains the same dangerous mask, predicting death—

the weakness, the emotion. They both hear the ticking of her watch on her slender wrist, cannon shots from an obsolete war, rumbling and exploding. He thinks: the hourglass has been turned over, I am beginning to empty. What do I know of her? She is much too strong. Or: fear hangs all around me, no one wants to notice because it is nothing, a fear of fans in a society drawing room. But I must take up my arms, this is the most dangerous, that she—

Then the animal wheels around, a flash of black lightning in the sky. The horns grip the *capa,* and he stands alone without weapons, an encounter with the sand. The blazing crowd. The huge body smells the victim and ah, ah, a tormented cry. He runs to the *barrera,* shadows fall across his gold, his *banderilleros* make the *quite.* The light stands like a pin in the big eyes of the body opposite him—

lets go of him, and the wild tumble begins, from the ship across the green water and the dancing Cyril all the way to his fears here. And the punishment on Schramm's loamy face, that he must work. What work? What? His helplessness unravels him; he knows he is exposed and unprotected. She sees how the insect lifts its legs in order to say something, and she says, "I want—

The *picadores* enter on their horses, raising their torturing sticks toward heaven. They turn and turn in the arena. The eyes in the mask follow the movements of the bull. The crowd chews, drinks, watches. The bull attacks, pushes and yanks with his horns at an anxious equestrian statue. The man on the horse sticks a *garocha* into the black hide, in the neck. Then there is blood. After the voluptuous gasp, whistling begins, interspersed with isolated shouts of abuse. The iron point penetrates farther into the flesh—

you to go away, to go away. It's impossible. I want to be alone here again." She opens her mouth to say more, the mouth that has bitten him, but she says nothing. He goes on staring at her face as if not seeing her. He wants to scream with revulsion at standing here with a stranger. Thinking, I don't know you, I don't know you, he says, "But I want to work, I know it was awful." But this is all

82

ridiculous, he does not have to say it. Her face becomes more hostile. He is seized by an overwhelming desire to humiliate himself, to crawl, to beg—

Has he been properly hit? The ritual hatred does not concern the man. He sees the small bloody pyramid reemerge from the black flesh and studies. There is still too much strength, too much strength. And incalculable cowardice. Again, the horse-filled mattresses begin to walk around. The mounted peasant, the man with iron feet, lifts the sharpened stick with which he will suck away the bull's strength. Ever slighter in his gold, the fighter peers out from behind his shield. The hatred of thousands now flows toward him, too—

There they stand in this grim situation, to be reviewed a thousand times. English truths rise like gases in his mind, all-explaining maxims that clarify and determine him, *there has been no joy*, like the balloon in a cartoon, that bubble full of words above their heads in which he needs only to grabble because they are there, *this is a naturalistic situation*, and the rhetoric works under its own power and outside the constant confirmation of this, goes on counting like a computer and collecting data, so as to examine him from all angles, really observe him everywhere, to enter, in the teeth, right in the middle. His legs will carry him to his cowardly sacrifice, he will execute those *particular* veronicas. The blood, syrup, flows, no, trickles, from the hairy plant, flank, it trickles in the sand and lies there, the voice of the public roars toward the President, that king in his *palco,* the hand waves from on high with the white handkerchief, the sweaty voices lie down. But the matador nods to the man on the blindfolded horse, and for the third time the iron is driven into the flesh, the multitude screams *"Fuera fuera* FUERA FUERA,*"* out, out, a repeatable situation. Because this at least: the space in which they stand, the corridor of her house, is square. He closes the door, they are alone—but really, he sees her, she sees him, from how many angles are they visible together? What is happening? How can I escape, he thinks, how can I escape her yet stay with her? How do I not lose, how may I be allowed to stay? He goes toward her through a beam of light that comes from the window above the door and is aimed at the floor, a footlight to where she is standing, but she retreats. He sees it clearly, her feet retreating, a caravan, and he follows her for several centimeters and says, "I have almost no money left. Wait until I have some money again, I won't trouble you." But her sternness increases. He sees in the green rays of her eyes—

the man standing in the shade, the man who has the function of a killer. This is not a real fight, it is enacted in shadows, he is a shadow of the shadow, the one who will kill, the one who observes. The sign with the handkerchief, the trumpets, the horses stumble toward the exit, walking like the exhausted beasts of a defeated army. He sees his dancing harpoonists enter, their shouts inciting the evading bull, the long arc, the hooking of the colorful, festooned lollipops into the hairy flesh. He looks and looks and sees his victim sagging feebly at the knees, and the organ begins again, *Otro toro otro toro otro toro*—

the hardness, the decision. "No," she says, "no, you can't stay. I want to be alone here again. And what you need, you can get easily enough on the island." "What do I want then?" he asks, but he knows that the answer she might give is the one he will never allow himself to consider clearly, because now she is insulting him and humiliating him with the truth. He goes toward her one more time, imploring, and touches her many times and taps her neck from behind and touches her head and pulls at her hands so that she will be the one who pulls him toward her. They fight in silence, briefly. Then with indifference she allows herself to be kissed by him and she—

Faena de matar. The act of killing. The light becomes more dangerous as he penetrates farther into the arena. He knows how he will now occupy himself. It has been shown. More and more, the animal becomes his own animal, his mirror. Toward that black mass, horns protruding like souls, he goes as if toward a mirror and looks into the gasping eyes. The next photographs become visible: all the sand, his right knee raised, on which floats a disc of gold, more and more reverently he kneels on his left knee. It is a scene of ineffable distinction. His pale face, in which the eyes of the photograph are blended with the eyebrows, or rather, the face with the holes, looks at the cloth raised perhaps as much as sixty centimeters into the air, hardened into iron. The animal drowns toward it. One of the lollipops hangs forward, broken, at the top of a broad band of greasy, minium-colored blood, the harbinger of death. The horns that will soon be dead. The blood that will soon be dead. The eyes that will soon be dead. The exploding sand. *Faena de matar*—

briefly takes him into her arms. What does she see? The stranger of that bright afternoon, which is still to begin, that afternoon, how long ago? Days that begin, and no one can see from how many kilometers' distance in time the taxi approaches from the town and pulls up at Marcos' terrace, the monumental taxi from which he steps, the hero of a story, the germs of fear in his body and decay in those same fingers with which he shakes hands with her, with which he now caresses her, the insane chemistry that changes everything, that operates and shifts in us—and he thinks, she sat there and we went to San Vicente, fragments of afternoon slip loose in his memory, and again he scratches and kisses her as on that first afternoon, and again decay slips through and she sees destruction sliding over his face like a cloth—

a different photograph. Death is coming closer. There is no tension at all in him. He will kill by looking, no, while looking. Looking replaces the real fighting, and fights. From this angle, it is as if the banderillas are coming out of the mouth, which drools a froth of blood. The front hooves are crazily raised toward him, but he holds the muleta like a spell of decay above the head in which the nostrils leer at the color like empty eyes, the color, always the lure of the color. *Mataló!* Kill him! But no, he will teach them, the heretics. This at last is the era of *punishment*—

and this frightens her. And at the same time as the fear, there comes, as always, contempt, but this time she does not push him away, she pulls him along out of the bathroom to the room where the bed is, and that is where he has to go, and suddenly he sees that he must do what he wanted to do, the comfort he wanted. He must now wind himself up, and he lies down and no longer holds her, no longer takes hold of her, but he lies there looking at the live beams on the ceiling and knows this is the worst she could do, this is punishment indeed. With an utmost effort of will, he rolls over toward her, toward that face, the masked head of a woman under him, all the hairs to be counted, all the eyelashes to be counted, light coming in through the windows and filling everything with hugely magnifying clarity. The cruelty in their eyes grows and grows—

the punishment that tames and pushes, lures and forces the animal back from the chosen battleground. Among the crowd, impatience bursts out afresh. The shouting seeps into him, he becomes more indifferent than ever. He looks at his victim. This is not difficult. Lifting the bloodstained cloth, he turns the animal into the desired position, places the sword in the air, straight ahead and as if it were supported by something, he leans against it, with all his strength. This is killing. The sword penetrates the flesh at a run and meets bone, like a silver particle of air it leaps up into the air. A hand gives him a new sword, but no, this monument is already dying, and how! A mouth full of blood lifted up to Zeus, a breath, the spirit, still bubbles through it, every bubble in that blood, every eruption in the minium. It is all called life, and here it dies, this life, black legs fold sideways, letting the body sink toward the golden sand where it wants to go, which it wants to paint. Look, it lurches sideways, in the small, predatorlike leap that death and life take together in that body, an electrocution, but he has long since turned away. The sun—

and sharpens itself on the actions they perform, for there is no other name for it. Then it is finished, *consummatum est,* and she has said a thousand times above him, I want you to go away, and has bitten the tears from his eyes with her teeth, removed them. She slides away from him, no longer touching him with her hands but pushing him away over her body so that her hands leave small, pitlike traces beside him in the mattress, and she raises herself in the corner and says mockingly, "And wept bitterly." He leaps up like a spring and bites her hand. With surprise she lifts that hand in the air and looks at the blood on it and kisses him, thereby dabbing a small amount of blood on his face, and says, "I can't help it, really I can't, we should never have started this." But this weakness more than anything destroys the other luxury of talking it out, and the pity that now begins—

has left the arena, only the *sol* seats are still lit by the sun, the heads of the *pobres* are still standing in light. In a wing of shadow he walks away, his gold no longer illumined. He disappears behind the redoubt of the *burladero*. While, amid cheers, the black thing is dragged away over the now-darkened sand, leaving a trail of gore, he feels an immense weariness, the accomplished deed, nestle inside him. His helper wipes the blood from his sword with a swift movement, some of the blood spatters on his hand, he sees it and does not see it. He knows it means something and vaguely thinks words of farewell, but this is going too far. No, he thinks, none of all this. Water washes the blood from his hand, and it vanishes, is no longer there—

pity! She has won the victory, now nothing is possible anymore. He lets her go and flees in utter despair into the corridor. Now to have to play-act . . . She pursues him with words, afraid of the ridiculous dialogue they pour out over each other, knowing that it is only a prolongation of something that is no longer there, that no longer exists.

They are standing in the corridor, chained, her hand with the blood on it raised in the air, a stage detail, and they both hear the hasty footsteps and know—North, and already that sample of American authorship stands before them, takes off its glasses in order to wipe the sweat out of its eyes, and they look at the panting blind man who stands there holding onto the doorpost. "Cyril has had a heart attack," he says to André. "He wants to see you."

"Why me?" he wonders and turns to her. Is she laughing?

She says, "I'll get someone to take your baggage to Schramm's. Is that all right?"

"You're bleeding, dodo," says North, and André sees the mysterious smile between those two, as if her hands had bled often in North's presence. Suddenly he thinks how little time he has been with her, how very much it was only a whim, a folly. Could there have been something between her and North? Or is something starting now?

"Are you coming with me?" he asks the American, who looks at him disdainfully and says,

"Come on, you papal placenta, this dead man won't bite

you," and after a moment's reflection, "Anyway, maybe he'll die while I am there. You know that the soul leaves the body at the moment when decay sets in. I'll wait for that." He takes off his spectacles, and again a blind man is speaking, his hand groping at the wall. "They say the soul is invisible. What do you think? But do get dressed now!" And as André gets dressed, he still hears behind him that grating voice speaking to her: "Did you love Cyril? I mean really, like I loved him? He was my favorite old man." And more softly, "Are you sending him away? Oh, oh! ah! I feel a cold wind! Cyril is dead! He came past here zzz through the passage, his soul knocked into the wall, well well. Hey, soul of Cyril, I can smell you, this soul smells of cheap Spanish brandy, Osborne-soul, Oxford-soul, platitude-soul, sweet-soul."

Standing in the passage, André sees how North wipes the blood from her hand with a handkerchief. "Why did he want to see me?" he asks.

North turns, looks at him, again too long. André lowers his eyes and hears North say, "No one will ever know why he wants to see you when he has had a heart attack. But everyone always wants to see you when they've had a heart attack. You understand? You have that special something, that something that is asked for at deathbeds. You could make a fortune just by kissing souls back to their places for one interminable second, because you can, Pacelli!" And kneeling on one knee, very rapidly: "And forgive us our mannerisms . . . Yo! putita de la Palabra, venga, hombre, venga! A taxi is waiting for us by the kiosk!"

Should he look at her, now that he is going away? He goes to her, cold demons holding him by the hand, a literary farewell. There he stands, bends down, kisses, his lips against her cheek, he has already gone, outside, goes down the hillside, past the cactuses, past the aloe, and she, standing in her doorway, watches them go, sees them disappearing into that arcadian bowl full of green with the Peloponnesian village, two former suitors descending the hillside and taking away different versions of her. It is unbearable.

She wants to shout herself free or kill herself out of their heads, out of their bodies, out of the memories in their hands and eyes, she wants to deny that which they possess of her, and she does not know whom she hates more, him she has defeated or North who will return.

She goes into the house and takes out of a drawer the portrait she has drawn of André, from a photograph, without his knowledge. Everything is in that face, the tissue of sentimentality and arrogance, the hatred he is scarcely aware of, on which he floats, and which destroys him precisely because he does not know it is hate and aggression that drive him. That is what he suffers from, she thinks. Go after him, make him come back, say I know I know, but no, tear up the portrait instead, black magic, and therefore at the same time be frightened of that deed and yet go triumphantly to the bathroom and write in pencil on the wall, cruelly, *nemo me inpune amavit,* nobody loved me with impunity. It is twelve o'clock in the morning, witching hour.

19

All this time they have not spoken. Once North stopped him and kissed him on the cheek. Tears sprang to his eyes. He remained silent until they reached the bottom of the hill and North did not rail at him but gave him another half embrace, the other half left hanging empty in the air. North told the taxi driver to hurry, the old car sighs and rattles past the now-familiar stations of the cross, the weathered mill, the house where apricots are dried, the hill with the ruin. North doesn't say much, perhaps he is affected after all. Once he asks how long André is thinking of staying on the island, and André says he will be leaving on the first available plane.

"Where to?"

"Back to Holland."

Holland! That ridiculous country that has never meant anything to him, that is where he suddenly wants to go, as if it would help. But he knows that he thinks it will help and that he therefore wants to go back, thinking his fear will diminish among the familiar—fatherland as remedy. Visions of heavy meadows and baleful summers . . . He feels more northern than ever and cloaks himself in nostalgia. They don't speak a word about Cyril. Does he hope he is already dead? In the distance, they see the familiar skyline, the town on the hill. The taxi drives straight to the Clínica. Who is sitting on the terrace? Not Cyril anymore!

A large Slavic-looking man takes them to the patient's room. *"Cuidado, eh? Y solamente uno puede entrar. Uno solo . . ."*

"Is he going to die?" asks North.

The man looks at him with sincere contempt and says, "Of course he is going to die. But he doesn't seem to mind, so you don't need to cheer him up, not him." And with rolling hips he goes down the corridor to his other dead.

North opens the door gently. Cyril's white head lies slumped forward. The yellowish hair has fallen over the left side of his face, and he looks like a very old, dirty girl. In the corner of his eye lies a tear. His lips bulge out slightly, and his eyes are only half-closed. White glassy shells stare into the room. One hand lies terribly alone on the thin white coverlet, the other is not there. André notices that North has to check a wave of nausea, but as he begins to walk toward the bed, across the swaying floor, he hears him hissing behind him, "Go greet the queen of all England, and be nice to him."

Get up, get up, he thinks as he stands by the bed and looks at the man lying in it. But the man does not move. An all-pervading urge to flee, to run away, overwhelms him. In an immense gaze, he takes in the room: the bleeding crucifix above the bed, and the bed itself, white enameled iron. Beside it, the locker with a book lying on it. A book! Under the bed an old suitcase covered in hotel stickers, Hotel Semiramis, Cairo. Hotel Damascus, Damascus. Hotel Beau Rivage, Nice. You'd never have thought it, would you, he says to the suitcase. Walking slowly toward the window, he looks out. In the garden, a nun is walking back and forth like an old upright animal that can read. Pace pace read read, her lips babble as she glides past the oleanders, clutching her little black book as though it were a prey. He taps on the window and she stiffens and stops and starts to look up, but he has already taken a step back and is standing behind the curtains, looking at her hand

90

and at Cyril's hand in turns, and thinking, that hand will wash this hand. From a vase on the floor he takes a flower and rubs one of its petals between thumb and forefinger, but no color comes off on his hand. Now the walls slowly begin to close in on him. Tilting, he walks backward to the door, but at that moment the old man lifts his eyelids, the pupils rise in the east and look at him. With the hand that is hidden under the blankets, Cyril pushes himself up. André clearly hears him say, "Welcome to my last universe, old chap. Nearer my God to Thee. Sit down." He points to the edge of the bed.

André sits down and comes closer to the sick man's face. There is a growth of long white hair on the dog-cheeks. They haven't shaved him. Perhaps it is no longer worth the trouble. Easier to shave a dead body?

In his overwrought state, he goes on tearing the flesh from Cyril's face and from his arms, those white, moving strips of cloth. He wants to see him dead and stiff already, in unseemly stillness in a coffin, because he knows it will happen anyway, soon, tomorrow. Therefore he says, leaning tensely toward the man in the bed, "And when are they letting you out again?"

The old man shakes with laughter, but it is a laugh with only a small margin for movement. The rest is squeaking and sighing. "Never! When I left London I knew I would return only as a corpse. Because I am going back, like a Chinese! Not because I care a damn, but because I want to . . . I know it doesn't mean anything, and yet it seems to be asking too much of me, all those rational notions . . . so . . . I don't want to lie here . . . lie here . . . on this island . . . hah . . . I am going home, a little trip by air. I have already fixed it with the consul."

Raising himself a little higher and therefore with a change of color in his face, "I don't know whether it is the . . . cloak of death that I now feel . . . ." He makes a gesture around him. "But I think I . . . it isn't what I had expected. There is no pathos. I try, but there is nothing. Do you know what I mean? No, you don't understand, at least you're not meant to understand. How is Clara?"

"All right."

"Are you still with her?"

91

He looks at the greedy curiosity in that face and thinks, how can you still act the lickerish old man on your deathbed? With some effort he says, "No, not any longer."

Cyril nods and slowly lets himself sink back in the pillows and turns over onto his side. Under a glass cover he would be one of those defiant waxwork saints in a Spanish cathedral, displayed for all eternity in divine deep-freeze, against infertility, against leprosy, against mental derangement. But no, once again the eyes spring open above the sagging cheeks and he says, with a little chuckle even, "All my life, especially when I was with a woman, I used to think, I wonder who will be my last woman. Infantile preoccupations! Not all that crazy, when you think of it. At any rate, it was *her* . . ."

He holds out his hand toward Cyril as if he really wanted to say something, but all he can think of takes the shape of her name. Clara, Clara.

"Are you sick?" (a dying man asks . . .)

"Yes."

"What is it that you have?"

"I don't know. I am sick."

Cyril moves his yellow finger over his forehead as if to sweep up a comforting thought from among the wrinkles. And as if to offer him the thought, he holds out his pointed fingers, as formerly he used to offer him shrimps or olives or a drink, and says, "Dying is a remedy for so much." But what does he mean? André wants to ask, what do you mean, but as a coda to the remark there now follows a nineteen-thirties movie-star sigh, and what is left of his eyes is raised toward heaven.

Dismayed, André clutches the edge of the bed and prays. "Not while I'm here! Let this cup pass me by!"

The eyes sink again and the mouth closes. Cyril is getting really tired now, and for the first time his visitor sees something that must be death creeping closer. Yet, even in his panic, he still manages to think about the body of this man and Clara. Cyril begins to talk again, but he does not listen, why should he listen? That life which is running out, which now tries to cover him with tatters of an English past, as if at this point he still wanted to render account, hurriedly put himself on the record, but it is in vain, the dying man has invited the wrong person, he may helplessly raise his eyes, sigh, smile, utter fragments of life, his visitor will hear it, but everything that is told here is someone else's life, he goes with him to Harrow, whispers a secret into the ears of Frieda Lawrence, fights at Passchendaele, sees the first movies of Valentino, the sails of the mill turn faster and faster, he puts on this runaway life like a new garment in order to keep his fear warm, and at the same time he still acts the part of listener at a deathbed, sitting like a mirror, as quietly as he can, and the old man shows himself that mirror and paints a whole lifetime on it. He, the mirror, absorbs it and thinks, pity I am not going to write anymore, pity, pity. Because I am not going to write anymore, I want to go away. With a not-to-be-shaken clarity it announces itself again. Beneath the drifts of life that now pass over him, the life of an Englishman, 1900—1962, which nestles inside him with stories about women, fears, survivals, he reads his own life, insofar as he has had one, and wants to go away. An orgy of fear and sorrow fills him, gone is that spell of clarity, as during that first night with Clara he feels he would like to roll about on the ground, howling and wailing, but with superhuman effort he holds himself in check. Don't wail, don't hit the dying man, don't run away.

All the temptations . . . all this emptying around him. But the doll, that body, is still there, something that is still present of the person he was, something that is busy driving life out of itself. It sits there and nods, the perfect listener, the deputy, the representative, nobody.

And the dying man, poor fellow, who had to be so cheated in his last few hours. A whole life full of real-life stories, valid for the last time and then never again, serving only to feed, to underline, someone else's fear. And still he is able to think!

A doctor enters. André does not hear what he says but tremblingly allows himself to be led away. But even before they reach the outer door, both he and the doctor are called back. There lies the dead man, his mouth slightly open, his hands dangling at the end of his outstretched arms. Our hero refuses the covering of the glassy gulls' eggs. Amid soothing noises he is taken to a room where a kindly nun (the one from the garden? No! She is washing Cyril, of course) gives him an injection. Thinking of the pain in his arm, he goes outside where the light begins to draw huge rays through him.

Now it is only a question of time.

20

At the junction of the two blocks of concrete, where the broad joints filled with soft tar crossed each other, the bird took wing and flew off as high as possible. He thought of the powders he had hidden deep down in his suitcase and watched the two *mozos* carrying the coffin to the plane. The group stood on the terrace by the bar, glasses in hand, sorrow on their faces. Only Pepe was seated, his wooden leg coquettishly stretched out before him, watching the swaying of the coffin with rapacious interest. When they reached the plane, a hole was opened in the silver wall of the old Bristol, a burial place. The *mozo* lifted the coffin with Cyril in it, very high, and shoved it into the pyramid. Thousands and thousands more layers of aircraft would have to be wrapped around it before he was buried, but the *mozo* looked unconcernedly across the cheap, crude wood at Antonio, his fellow-bearer, as if he was in the habit of loading English corpses into planes every day. Not so, Antonio! Masks of sorrow. These are observations, he thought. The injections, for which, since that first occasion, he had gone back many more times, always with long sob stories, soundlessly performed their duty. Disguised as himself, he sat at the edge of the airfield like a waiting fisherman. The blood moved slowly and thickly through its tunnels, and with effort he refocused his eyes on the cluster of greeters that had, as usual, gathered at the airport in order to drink and wave, but this time for a dead body.

He felt desperate, but it was a despair that no longer flared up. He was paralyzed, the protagonist in a tragic history. The compulsory thoughts as to what Cyril now looked like, whether he lay crookedly or oddly or contortedly because Luís had lifted him so high. Weeping, Antonio pushed his great English friend into the plane, his suitcase after him, and then turned in the blinding sunlight to the seaward side of the airfield where the Mediterranean bliss lay ready to hand, gleaming and glittering, the green, invisible hills beneath, the urns, the tangled seaweed, and the immortal fishermen sailing over it all, digging for treasure in the water, for living silver. André shivered with real sorrow. It was as with the moon, darkness was advancing, more and more light was being eaten away from him. He stood up and sat down again. North came toward him, but he had become invulnerable. The contempt he had for himself exceeded everything else. He looked into the face that seemed strange and insignificant to him and saw that it said Clara had come.

He looked at her. She approached. That chalk on her face is also grief. Why? Not for him who was going away, whom she had scarcely known, only two days. Or was it? Or for Cyril and what he took from her to where she will never be able to retrieve it? The memory of her had died, she had died. For herself then. He pitied her but could no longer join her. Under her eyes there was a hint of black. Her father had no doubt been shot by the partisans: together with her mother, she hid in the coach house. The servants fled.

She kissed him fleetingly, a kiss to bygones. For a moment he had a feeling that now he would have to get up and go with her, but the thought merely caused a slight gasp, and he looked at her, startling her. "I am going away," he said, while saying other things, pulling their relationship open and peering into it with all his strength, and he lifted his hands, which for more than fifty years had ruled the bishopric, and briefly rubbed her shoulder, the roundness of her shoulder. No irony at all, he thought, nothing, nowhere, the actors all found dead in bed, how about that?

One propeller of the old-fashioned plane started rotating, the silver machine shook, he became frightened again. Aviación y Comercio, S. A. Barcelona. In that adornment I shall fly. An ecstasy, but without any of the lightness that should accompany it, occupied him utterly, he was busy. But he saw her! Slowly, and at least twenty times, he stood up and walked past the guard of honor to the plane. Schramm, where is Schramm? And the doctor who said to him, *"Mejor que vuelva Usted inmediatamente a su país. Usted está ya muy enfermo* very, very ill," and the porous Catalan face had quivered, but not the hands . . . Schramm, Schramm? The painter dived across him, pushed him forward with a prod in the vertebrae, comforting him. He felt his eyes filling with tears. Schramm talked to him softly, blew and shoved him into the plane, and from behind the little windows he saw them all once again, the whole army. The plane trembled restlessly, but he kept looking as if he would never be able to see anything else again. There they stood, first the blue sky, dripping all around them, in which they floated, the painter and Clara. Her green eyes hung in the middle of her face and saw the blind window behind which he sat. She would never see him again.

Once more he fell from the hill with her and bit her in the neck, slept with her, but the malevolent shadow of North was slid between them, and nothing remained of her but the anger, the resistance. And Cyril wasn't there to wave goodbye to him! North said something to her and she laughed. What did he say, he would never know, what did North say? *Sujétense los cinturones . . .* your safety belts! But who was that coming toward the plane at this late hour? Charlie who walked on crutches and had once played the fiddle at Pepe's, supported by his gray wife. Cyril's friend . . . "I was in the Colonial Office. Why, Andrew, you must come to my *finca* one day, Cyril knows where to find it, it is near Santa Gertrudis, there is no light and no water, of course, but I even grow figs! *Higos . . .*" They would all die separately, wasn't that an exciting thought? Owing to the trembling of the plane, the coffin shifted in the baggage hold. Looking behind him he saw it. *Sujétense los cinturones. Prohibido fumar.* The only other passenger, an old Spaniard in white shoes, made the sign of the cross, scared, and rightly so. The plane begins to scream and run, into the sea, look! the town, look! the island, and he hangs above the island. His beloved is now very small, and he cannot see her anymore. On the sea sails a white ship, the ship from Barcelona? Is he on it? He himself once more on the way to his arrival!

From on high he peers at his image. The body in the coffin in

96

the baggage hold has once again become human and stands in tweeds by the rail, talking to him. Does time care? Everything happens always, constantly. Like a thread, he is being pulled through the needle of his fate, the plane dips briefly to greet the ship, it really is the same ship, the *Ciudad de Valencia,* the air displaced by the dip rises forcefully in his body, a dizziness swirls behind his eyes, but he goes on looking until the ship disappears behind the plane, and then there is nothing left but the sea, a gleaming sheet, and the shadow on it, a small advancing shadow, and he is in it, and so is Cyril. The shadow makes a sound, a low rumble with a high whine in it. He lights a cigarette and puts it out again. In vain he tries to order his thoughts, but every thought is engulfed by hundreds of overwrought images and every one of these images he interrupts with the panacea: go home, to Holland. And at the same time, a nostalgia out of all proportion, but for what? Schramm, her, the island, because he would have wished to be healthy and lie on the rocks, wear light blue clothes and get brown, the most childish of wishes, behind which disaster lurks. In the slow arc drawn by the plane he sees the island once again but now so immensely far away, shadowy hills floating in a haze, it cannot be true that this has anything to do with the reality of his past, and images, nothing but images come thronging forward, ever more cunningly, bits of wall, leaves of plants, a tile in her bathroom, a name on a piece of paper, a glass in a hand, but whose hand? The island becomes one with the sea, floats away, but they are there, where he sees nothing anymore. They are there and he is here. He thinks he says aloud I want to go back, but he says it so softly that the old Spaniard does not hear him. Then he goes to the small toilet and waits in his cell until he feels the nausea of the descent and returns to earth in the form of a victim.

The mud-colored city, cut into squares, lands alongside the plane. He hurries down the steps into the steaming light and stands on a floating block of concrete. He sees two workmen in blue overalls climb into the plane and hears their exclamation as they see the coffin. They re-emerge with grave faces and deposit the coffin on the concrete. They have not known Cyril, he is being

97

declassed as dead. No one comes to meet André. He has promised the British consul on the island to make sure the coffin is put on a plane to England.

After a shy glance at the coffin, the old Spanish gentleman has vanished. The workmen have walked away, gesticulating, their faces suddenly piss-colored in the sun, the wooden mask of the sudden fright already gone. Slowly he beings to walk away from the coffin which, still and very lonely, remains standing under the silver plane.

"Goodbye, Cyril," he says softly and starts to run. At the end of the concrete area he looks back once more. The plane, the coffin. There it stands, a small wooden thing, nobody near it, Cyril inside. He opens his mouth to say something to a man in a peaked cap, but long, woolen threads bubble out of his mouth, no words, no message. A terrible dryness hangs on his tongue, between his teeth. He looks helplessly at the man, at the coffin, at the body he can see through the wood. The steps he now takes, backward, take a long time. He has to pull himself away from the ground, at each new step farther away, but no one goes to the coffin. And the pilots, haven't they come out of the plane yet? Who is to look after Cyril? He takes three, four quick steps and stretches out one arm, which is left hanging in the chemical heat. "No," he says, "uh." There are no people on the airfield, only planes. Not one goes to the coffin. Then he turns and runs for a taxi.

He lets himself fall on the back seat. The driver does not ask him where he wants to go, just starts driving toward the city. Once more he looks, through tears, through water, at the coffin immobile on the concrete. Then a bend in the road cuts even that away, and a new guilt has entered him, pursues him with the others. And in what kind of terrain!

Landscape, landscape. He closes his eyes. When they enter the city, at which he does not want to look, he asks to be taken to the Estación de Francia. The ticket window he wants, "Países Extranjeros," is closed. *Cerrado.* Moving with difficulty through the swollen coolness, he goes to the Informaciones RENFE. Red Ferrocarriles Reales de España. Or *Reunidos?* Not until tomorrow can he buy a ticket, *a las ocho de la mañana. Seguro? Sí, hombre, sí!* But he knows he will not go tomorrow. I daren't go in a train, I'll fall out. Another taxi takes him to a hotel, Schramm has given him the name. It is somewhere behind the Ramblas. He hands in his baggage and at once goes into town. He can't lie or sit any longer. All the time he thinks of Cyril, then of her, of her on that island, which is nearer than the Netherlands, and to which he wants to return. He decides to go back the following day, whatever they will say there. Shyly, nervously, he moves through the overtures of his death, for will it be this afternoon? He wanders about the city, goes to the park high up in the hills, lies under trees, but the same restlessness and a new one drive him farther and farther. Scurrying down paths, he repeats his decision a thousand times as if on a prayer mill, tomorrow I am going back to the island, then I will start working. But he has to say it again and again, in order not to forget it, for images of mortal terror and long-winded English phrases are forming in his head, phrases that detach the terror like incantations but that lead nowhere and deliver him up again: "Now he himself was never . . . Therefore he would remember, this sophisticated, fisticated, never united . . . what? Brr, and in the sweet mountains . . ." Someone asks him for a light, and with shame he asks himself whether the man will think he is mad because he is talking aloud to himself. Or is he not talking aloud to himself? Or is he mad? Take a deep breath.

Cool air from under the trees. Evening is coming, soon it will be evening. Then he must go to bed. He doesn't want to. Then it will grow dark outside, then the terror within will win. He breathes in the air with a whistle and blows it out again. The evil goes out with it, that which threatened him . . . he gives it back. Only when it really grows dark does he take a taxi back to the city.

21

What a tangle of lies and deceit I have created . . . and how strong does he emerge from it! As the writing proceeded he caught up with me, this book was his idea; my lesser nerves, my smaller capacity for the extreme, for what he called suffering, complete it.

Exactly in the way he foresaw and intended it. For while I was writing the last chapter, I began to wonder more and more often whether he had not deliberately shunted me onto this track: he starts on a book about a writer who writes about a writer who dies, and he himself dies before he has completed the book about the dead writer. André Steenkamp did not manage to finish his book, but with my help he brings it off after all, for he knew exactly to whom to leave his papers. Of course, it is a rather drastic way of writing books, but with the help of someone like me he succeeded. These are the last pages, I now need only to let him die. Or not? I went to see the hotel room where it happened, in Barcelona. Also the cemetery where he was buried, but I did not find his grave, did not want to find it, though I would have liked to take a walk around that cemetery together with him. Monstrous mausoleums, storage chests with pillars and angels the color of excrement. And carved into the stone, names that have become null and void, names that have to denote corpses and perished rags. But his resting place was less distinguished. I had to climb and climb through urban conglomerations for the dead, cheap real estate, up a long asphalt road lined with black-haired trees, until I reached the shelves of bodies, the tenement blocks. Unending rows, clawing higher and higher into the sky, divided into compartments. In every one of these lies a body hidden behind the painted words AQUÍ DEPOSITO EL CADAVER DE . . . here lies deposited the body of André Steenkamp. I didn't want to see that. I have had far too much to do with him these two years that I penetrated into the last few overwrought weeks of his life. Has he got me by the throat? There is no doubt that I have reconstructed him differently from the way he was, this dead man, any more than it can be doubted that he was stranger than I am making him out to be. True, he died of it, of that ridiculous life he led, but on the other hand he had engineered it rather cleverly, that book, right till the very end, including me.

His hero had to die (*his* notes) after the manner of Louis Couperus' heroine, Eline Vere. I admit that I have not managed that. I already had a dead Cyril, he was one too many. Moreover, it was clear that he was already destroyed. But even if I had wanted it, I would not have succeeded. Eline Vere . . .

"*'Se in tanto affa . . . a . . a . . . anno!'* she murmured, almost weeping, in doleful cadences, and her soul's sorrow grew and her wails rose higher and higher: *'Non son degna di pietá!'*

"She started vehemently, aghast at the shrieking, penetrating sound of her broken voice, and she cast the bedcover aside and sat up, trembling. She sobbed but laughed at the same time, she laughed at herself. If she became thus agitated she would never sleep. Brusquely she threw herself on the disordered bed and closed her eyes. But sleep did not come. 'O God!' she groaned. 'God! Let me sleep, I implore thee, let me sleep.' And she wept bitterly, incessantly. Then a thought flashed through her brain. If she drank a few drops more than the doctor from Brussels had prescribed?"

What should I have done with this? Copy it, or the surrounding passages, and paint him into the picture, heroically? I have always hated the manner of his dying. If you are so sure of your case you should bring fate into it, let planes crash, attract drunken drivers or avalanches toward yourself, anything. Not that inextricable shadow play in dusky hotel rooms. An insignificant life, I said at the beginning, and a love, or whatever it was, that finally emptied it. Was that how it was? Do I know it now, now that I have reached the end of my reconstruction? What am I to say? Now that I have come to these pages, it is suddenly as though *I* had to render an account of his death. But that was never my intention. His death was there. I had to make *him* precede it. But surely I did not have to say who he was? In any case, anything I might want to try in that way would become an even worse lie, but I don't want to try, I want to get rid of him. The Knight has died. This is only his testament.

Of course I know how he died, the green-sickly face raised to the clouded hotel room ceiling, a stupefying, drifting death, a sleep that I do not even imagine as unpleasurable, for at last something was being done, it began to throb, at any rate. The notion that he ought really to have been born at that moment cannot have oc-

101

curred to him, he was too busy listening to the gravediggers' spades. That is how I let him die, how he died. The rest others must do. Whatever I might try, I would all the time be writing the same book. Why? Because this is not finished. It is not finished, he is not *dead*. He still roams around in his papers, a blind man unable to see himself. He has not recognized himself, I have made no mirror for him. He still does not know himself and refuses to be killed, refuses to be sent to the land of heroes. But I have done my duty. Now that I have come to the end, there is nothing left for me but fear and revulsion, perhaps even hatred. Even if I were to write the words *The End* under it a thousand times, it would still not be finished. The title is an announcement, not reality. Of course he is dead. But that is not what his book was called. I had to make him die. Instead of which, I drive him into his hotel, murder him, slam the lid of his coffin with a bang! I have failed. I do not know who he was.

So, dear friend, let someone else embroider you in your death. Let him take what he wants from these papers. Don't bother me anymore, but leave me in peace. Bother *her,* or your friends North and Schramm, or haunt, together with Cyril, the island where you, more than anyone, belonged. I don't want to anymore. I free myself from your deadly embrace and put you away. It has not happened. I am the one who flees.

AQUI DEPOSITO EL CADAVER DE ANDRÉ STEENKAMP